ANCIENT SENTINEL

ANCIENTS RISING SERIES
BOOK SEVEN

KATIE REUS

Cover Art by Sweet 'N Spicy Designs
Editor: Julia Ganis
Author Website: https://katiereus.com

Publisher's Note: This is a work of fiction. Names, characters, places, and incidents are either the products of the author's imagination or used fictitiously, and any resemblance to actual persons, living or dead, or business establishments, organizations or locales is completely coincidental.

Ancient Sentinel/Katie Reus.—1st ed.

ISBN: 978-1-63556-214-9

PRAISE FOR THE NOVELS OF
KATIE REUS

"...a wild hot ride for readers. The story grabs you and doesn't let go."
—*New York Times* bestselling author, Cynthia Eden

"Has all the right ingredients: a hot couple, evil villains, and a killer
action-filled plot. . . . [The] Moon Shifter series is what I call Grade-A
entertainment!"
—Joyfully Reviewed

"I could not put this book down. . . . Let me be clear that I am not saying
that this was a good book *for* a paranormal genre; it was an excellent
romance read, *period.*"
—All About Romance

"Reus strikes just the right balance of steamy sexual tension and nail-
biting action....This romantic thriller reliably hits every note that fans
of the genre will expect."
—*Publishers Weekly*

"Prepare yourself for the start of a great new series! . . . I'm excited
about reading more about this great group of characters."
—Fresh Fiction

"Wow! This powerful, passionate hero sizzles with sheer deliciousness. I
loved every sexy twist of this fun & exhilarating tale. Katie Reus
delivers!"
—Carolyn Crane, RITA award winning author

"A sexy, well-crafted paranormal romance that succeeds with smart
characters and creative world building."
—Kirkus Reviews

"You'll fall in love with Katie's heroes."
—*New York Times* bestselling author, Kaylea Cross

"Both romantic and suspenseful, a fast-paced sexy book full of high stakes action."
—Heroes and Heartbreakers

"Katie Reus pulls the reader into a story line of second chances, betrayal, and the truth about forgotten lives and hidden pasts."
—The Reading Café

"Nonstop action, a solid plot, good pacing, and riveting suspense."
—RT Book Reviews

"Exciting in more ways than one, well-paced and smoothly written, I'd recommend *A Covert Affair* to any romantic suspense reader."
—Harlequin Junkie

"Sexy military romantic suspense."
—USA Today

"Enough sexual tension to set the pages on fire."
—*New York Times* bestselling author, Alexandra Ivy

"*Avenger's Heat* hits the ground running...This is a story of strength, of partnership and healing, and it does it brilliantly."
—Vampire Book Club

"*Mating Instinct* was a great read with complex characters, serious political issues and a world I am looking forward to coming back to."
—All Things Urban Fantasy

CHAPTER ONE

A s Grace reached the bottom step into the foyer, her sister Luna was stepping out of the living room. She narrowed her eyes at her sister and a split second later they both sprinted for the kitchen.

"Ha!" Grace made it inside a moment before Luna—and found their older sister Jo, and Jo's mate Cas, making out by the coffee pot. "Ugh, you guys!"

Luna sidestepped her and practically shoved Jo and her dragon mate out of the way as she dove for the pot. "Snooze you lose, sucker," she said, practically cackling as she started pouring herself the last of the coffee pot.

Grace glared at her sister, no heat behind it. "At least start another pot." She was verging on whining but didn't care. She needed coffee stat —because she was on a mission.

Today was *the* day.

Yep. It definitely was.

Grace was tired of ignoring her feelings for her friend Ren, tired of pretending they didn't exist. She needed to get whatever this weirdness was *out* of her system. Which meant she actually needed to talk to Ren. And then maybe…get him inside her. Which sounded super dirty but whatever. She wasn't going to get over the jaguar shifter anytime soon.

Not when she saw him practically every day—and wanted way more than friendship.

Before all that, however, she needed coffee. Her liquid courage to pump her up.

"You're such a baby," Luna grumbled, practically shoving her mug at her, but her mouth curved up into a grin. "I know you need it more than me, especially today."

"Why especially today?" Cas frowned as he looked between the two of them.

Grace inhaled deeply, took a sip of the perfectly doctored coffee. She and Luna drank it exactly the same, because they were both awesome. Three sugar scoops and two pours of creamer. Well, milk, since that was all they could get after The Fall. After taking a sip, she shrugged at her brother-in-law.

"Come on, why?" He looked at Luna now.

"None of your business," Luna said with a grin as she started scooping out coffee grounds for a new pot.

"I'm part of the family now." The giant dragon looked almost hurt as he glanced between all three of them, his gaze landing on his mate. "Don't I get to know family stuff?"

Jo's eyes were wide as she looked at Grace, her expression pleading. "Come on, he's not going to say anything."

"Fine, but keep it zipped." She motioned a zipper across her lips. "And no big brother over-the-top stuff, okay?" She'd quickly learned that once he was officially mated to Jo, he'd slid into a protective big brother role with ease—and dragons were already overprotective on a regular day.

He frowned, but nodded.

"I'm going to maybe...see if..." She cleared her throat.

"Oh my God, she's going to put herself out there with Ren," Luna said in exasperation.

His frown deepened as he slid a casual arm around Jo, pulled her close.

Grace was so glad her older sister had found such happiness—and with the sweetest, if deadly, dragon.

"Put yourself out there?" he asked.

Jo nudged him. "She's going to make a move on him."

"I'm not making a move. I'm just...testing the waters. Seeing if maybe he's interested in me." She was still figuring out the logistics. Because she'd never actually asked a guy out. Men or males had always asked her out. But she was impatient and needed to know if the spark she felt for him was just one-sided. The uncertainty was killing her.

"He's interested." Cas nodded in assurance. "Most definitely."

"Really?" The jaguar was impossible to read. He was around all the time, the best listener, but...he'd never, *ever* made a move, or even hinted at wanting her. And from what she understood of shifters, they had no problem just going for what they wanted. Cas was a little different in that he'd been worried about how Jo would react to the knowledge that he was a dragon—since their parents had been killed by dragons in The Fall. He'd dragged his feet making a move.

But Grace had never doubted that Cas was into Jo. Yet even though Grace had been around shifters for a while now, she was still human. It wasn't as if she could scent Ren or anything so she felt as if she was at a disadvantage. Like, maybe she was missing something.

"How do you know?" Luna asked as she waited for the fresh pot of coffee to percolate.

Cas blinked. "Ah...I just do."

Grace sighed. That was not helpful and she didn't want to waste any more time, especially since she had off work today. "Thanks, Cas." She patted his forearm gently, then hugged both her sisters. "Wish me luck."

Butterflies were basically living inside her as she grabbed her bicycle and headed out. After The Fall most people in the New Orleans territory either walked or biked. There were still cars—though they were all magically powered for the most part. But Grace liked biking everywhere, had painted her bike neon purple and teal and had a wire basket in the front that held anything she needed. She stayed within the territory for the most part, and if she needed to go anywhere too far she had friends she could ask for a ride. Or heck, Cas could just fly her if she was desperate.

She'd adjusted to this new life fairly quickly, embraced it really. Her

Irish grandmother would have it no other way. *You pivot in life if necessary or you are destined to be miserable.* One of her grandmother's common sayings.

Something Grace wholeheartedly believed. Which was why she was kicking her own butt for waiting so long with Ren. It had only been months but still, she knew how fragile life was. If he didn't want anything more than friendship with her, then she'd deal.

Or…she'd drown herself in ice cream.

Whatever.

But she needed to know.

Today was one of those perfect spring days, flowers blooming and birds chirping like little demons as she made her way through the Garden District. The closer she got to the home Ren shared with his two friends Griff and Hyacinth, the more her anxiety ratcheted up.

What was she even going to say to him? Ask him out? That was…a foreign concept to her. And how would he know she meant for a date anyway? She'd have to specify, and the thought of his rejection was terrifying.

She now lived in a world where she was aware of actual dragons—she lived in the same house with one—and the male she was seriously obsessed with could turn into a deadly jaguar, but she was more scared of his rejection.

"You've got problems," she muttered to herself as she biked by a park filled with kids and parents. A few cubs were in animal form, wolf mostly, utilizing the jungle gym, and it was beyond adorable. She loved seeing all the species interacting, knew that this territory had fared a lot better than many. At least that was what she'd been told from friends in other territories.

As a plant geneticist, her professional circle was small and she was thankful that many of her friends had survived The Fall as well. Strokes of luck more than anything—they'd been in the right territory at the right time. Her parents hadn't and…that was something she wasn't going to think about.

Not today when she was feeling wild and brave.

And terrified.

She forced herself to slow her pedaling as she reached the crosswalk before Ren's street. Maybe…she would just see if he wanted to go for a walk or have brunch or…something. She'd figure it out.

As she passed people she recognized, she waved, breathing in the scent of the magnolia trees, grounding herself. It didn't help much; her heart rate kicked up a thousand beats as she reached the end of the street.

Only one more left turn and then his house was two down. She was almost there. And now she was worried he'd be able to hear her crazy heartbeat.

Wait, could shifters do that? Oh no, she wasn't sure. She knew they could scent stuff, so she was really careful to keep her thoughts in check when she was around Ren. Which was a major effort in self-control.

When she felt her phone buzz multiple times in her back pocket, she stopped and leaned her bike against a nearby oak tree and pulled it out.

Go get some! From Luna.

Then, *You got this!* from Jo, a few seconds later.

She laughed when even a text from Cas popped up. Though his was much more formal. *You should not lack in confidence, little sister. You can do this.*

Dang it, now she really couldn't chicken out. She was just gonna rip off the bandage. Tell Ren how she felt, that she liked him. *Liked* him, liked him.

Heart still a wild beat in her chest, she left her bike where it was and headed down the sidewalk. As she approached, she saw Ren step outside his home through a cluster of azalea bushes blooming pretty pinks.

Yep, her heart was going to explode at this point. Tall and lean with bronze skin and a charming, easy smile, Ren was gorgeous. She hadn't even noticed him the first night he'd been at her family's house, but she'd sure noticed him later when he'd saved her from a crazy vampire. And she'd been noticing him ever since.

She took a step forward, raised her hand to call out to him, but froze when she realized he wasn't alone.

A tall female with jet-black hair was with him, turning toward him… hugging him.

5

And Ren was hugging her back, the embrace looking so intimate. As if...the female had stayed the night. It was pretty early, and there was no reason for a female to be at his place so early other than one thing.

Throat tight, she took a step back, feeling foolish. Of course he was seeing someone. Look at him, of course he was.

She was just grateful she hadn't made a fool of herself, told him how much she thought about him, dreamed about him...freaking obsessed about him.

Blinking away tears, she quickly backtracked and jumped onto her bike. She was too embarrassed to go home now.

She needed to ride around for a while until she could face her sisters, tell them how wrong and stupid she'd been.

How very, very stupid. Her chest ached as she rode blindly down the street, desperate to simply put distance between them. She'd built up a connection in her head, had somehow thought he was into her. She'd seen a few covert looks from him and had thought...

It didn't matter. Not one little bit. Because clearly she'd been wrong. He was seeing someone—and the female was gorgeous at that. Was probably a shifter too.

Grace knew she couldn't compete, and was angry at herself for thinking she had a chance with a male like Ren. She wasn't quite thirty yet and Ren was at least over a hundred years old. He'd probably done and seen more than she could imagine. Of course he wasn't interested in her.

As another wave of tears threatened, she decided to head home after all. She wanted to curl up in her room and block out everything for a while.

CHAPTER TWO

A t the soft knock on her bedroom door, Grace knew who it was. Mainly because Jo and Cas were gone for the evening and so was her grandmother Josephine. "You can come in."

Luna stuck her head in, her emerald green eyes, the same shade as Grace's, wide. "You want company?"

"Sure." She paused the movie she was watching—they didn't have streaming or anything like that anymore, but she still had a handful of DVDs. "What's up?"

Luna pushed the door fully open and then picked up a tray of…two cups of what were likely hot cocoa and other snacks.

Oh hell, she could feel those dumb tears coming on again. "What's all this?"

"Figured it was a good night for some hot chocolate and old movies."

"I thought you had plans?"

"Eh." Luna shrugged and moved into the room, set the tray on the tufted bench at the end of the bed before she picked up one of the mugs. "I'd rather hang out with you," she said as she handed Grace the cup.

"I want to tell you to go out but I'm feeling lonely and selfish," she admitted.

"It's not selfish to want to be with family."

"You're starting to sound like Nana."

"Who has more of a life than us," Luna said on a laugh as she joined her on the bed and kicked her panda-sock-covered feet out.

Grace snickered as she took a sip of her drink, sighed in appreciation. "Want to watch this, or I can put in a different movie?"

"Maybe something Christmasy even though it's spring?"

"Sounds good to me. You pick."

Luna slid off the bed again. "You just don't want to get out of bed."

Grace snickered again because it was true.

"So…I'm not trying to kill you with questions," Luna said as she started perusing the movie boxes, even though she knew exactly what Grace had. "There's a chance that he wasn't, like, you know, with someone else. I mean, you didn't see him kissing her or anything, right?"

Grace took another sip, ignored the way her stomach tightened. "They were hugging—embracing. It looked very…intense. There's no other word for it." And she wished she could unsee it. "Look, it's fine. I'm going to be fine. I'm just having a pity party for myself tonight but I'll be back to normal tomorrow." That was a big fat lie, but whatever. She was allowing herself to wallow and just veg tonight.

Luna made a sort of clucking sound with her tongue as she slid another movie into the DVD player. "Hugging isn't kissing, and I don't know if I'm fully on board with the thought of him—"

"Luna. I know you mean well and I love you, but trust me, it's okay. He's obviously dating someone. I knew it was going to happen sooner or later. I just thought I had a chance." Clearly she'd been wrong, but at least she hadn't confessed her feelings to him.

Silver linings and all that.

Luna simply shrugged and slid into bed. As she did, Grace heard her phone buzz, paused when she saw Ren's name on the screen.

Hey, headed out soon, wanted to see if you wanted to join? Dinner, drinks, maybe dancing at Cynara's club.

She blinked, then held up her phone so Luna could read it.

Luna blinked too, snatched the phone from her and texted like a madwoman before Grace could snatch the phone back. By the time she'd set her mug down with her other hand, Luna cackled manically and tossed it to her.

Can't tonight, have a date, but have fun! See you later this week. Then she ended it with some kissy face emojis.

Grace's mouth fell open as she reread the message. "What the hell, Luna!"

Her sister laughed even harder. "Whatever. Now he knows you're dating too."

Little bubbles popped up, then disappeared, then popped up, then disappeared again. Then nothing. "I should just tell him that was you who texted."

"No way." Luna grabbed the phone, slid it onto the nightstand on her side of the bed. "Let me have this. You know you want to anyway."

"I don't like lying," she grumbled, but yeah, okay, her sister wasn't wrong. She liked the thought of him thinking she was dating too.

She should be getting out there anyway. She knew enough about shifters that if he was dating, it would be serious or heading that way. The majority of shifters she knew were wired differently than most humans—monogamy and possessiveness were the norm.

"Just enjoy the movie and put him out of your mind for tonight." Luna grabbed the remote and pressed play.

And Grace knew better than to argue with her youngest sister.

REN STARED AT HIS PHONE, blinked once, twice.

"What did that phone do to piss you off?" Griff murmured as he stepped into the kitchen, dressed as if he was ready to head out for the night.

Ren turned away from the sink, feeling off-kilter. "She's going on a date."

"Who?"

"Grace."

"With you?"

"No, dumbass. Or I wouldn't be pissed."

Griff's eyes widened as he grabbed a beer from the fridge. One of their neighbors was into brewing and had been giving them tons of free samples. "Sorry, man. I did tell you not to get tangled up with a human."

"Really? You're giving me an 'I told you so' now?"

Griff winced. "Sorry, I'm a dick. I'm just all up in my head today. It's been a long one. I...am surprised she's going on a date with someone else. I thought you two were moving... I'm really sorry."

Ren scrubbed a hand over his face. "She texted me like it's no big deal so I guess... Hell." He shoved his phone in his back pocket. "I can't follow her on her date and kill the guy, right?"

"I can't actually tell if you're joking. And the answer is no."

He rolled his eyes. "Where's Hyacinth? I need to talk to her." Their other roommate would back him up.

"She's with Thurman tonight, and no, you're not talking to her. She'll condone violence and that's a mistake—and I'm still going to assume you're joking. Because you can't kill someone for going out with Grace."

Ren's jaguar side begged to differ. He kept that thought to himself, however. "What are you up to tonight?"

Griff shrugged. "Hanging with the tiger twins. They want to spar, go running...and honestly, I feel like they need a chaperone sometimes."

Ren snorted. Harlow and Brielle—the tiger twins—were felines, so yeah, a chaperone was a good thing. Tigers were beyond mischievous, and that was saying something considering he was a jaguar. "Are you meeting them at their place?"

"Yeah. You wanna come with?"

He nodded, fighting the ever-present possessiveness over Grace that had swelled inside him.

"Wait, are you hoping to ask about Grace, see if they know who she's dating?" Griff narrowed his gaze as they headed out the side door and into the cool night air.

"What?" Ren snorted, as if the thought was ridiculous.

"Do I need to chaperone you tonight?" Griff's tone was dry.

Ren just grinned even as his jaguar swiped at him. She was on a date —and hadn't even hinted that she was seeing someone. It had to be new. He'd just seen her yesterday. He'd met her after work, walked her home

—had dinner with her when her nana asked him to stay over. Then he and Grace had enjoyed drinks out on her front porch. She'd mentioned nothing about dating.

"Oh goddess, you're going to get me killed," Griff muttered.

Ren simply shoved his hands in his pockets as they strode down the sidewalk.

"So I heard Destiny stopped by this morning. How is she?"

Ren's mood immediately shifted, a different kind of protectiveness swelling up. "Good. Or as well as possible, considering. She decided to stay in the territory and has met Prima—who's helping her learn to defend herself, to fight." Ren wanted to wrap the young woman in cotton, keep her safe from the world. But that was impossible and she had to learn how to protect herself.

"Good." There was a bite of savageness to Griff's words.

And it mirrored the way Ren felt. Destiny was one of the humans who'd been kidnapped by vampires and held against her will, along with a whole host of other humans. What the vampires had done to those females… He rolled his shoulders as another pop of rage surfaced. Ren had killed some of them, had been part of the team that rescued them. Some humans had chosen to return to their territories and others had chosen to stay. "It's a long road, but she's got a strong will. I think she'll eventually be truly okay."

Griff nodded. "I'm glad. I just wish it had never happened at all."

Yeah, so did Ren and anyone with an ounce of empathy. The Alpha of this region was solid, a good male down to his core, and he'd made sure that anyone involved in the trafficking ring had been killed or imprisoned. It never should have happened here—or anywhere—but sometimes evil slipped into the crevices and found a way.

The walk to the twins' place didn't take long and Ren was surprised to see Aurora and King leaving as he and Griff headed up the driveway. The Alpha couple were always busy, but Aurora had once lived here with her pack before mating with King. And Ren knew that she visited more often than not.

"Hey, you two," Aurora said, a big smile on her face. Her phoenix wings were glowing tonight, on full display—a rarity, he knew.

King simply nodded at them, his expression more reserved.

"If I may risk losing my head, you look stunning tonight," Griff said, slightly bowing at Aurora.

King's mouth kicked up a fraction.

"Thank you," Aurora said, beaming. "I engaged in a flying contest tonight and decided to stretch my wings for a while."

"Who challenged you?" Ren couldn't keep the surprise out of his voice.

"Hunter." King's tone was dry.

Hunter was their pet dragonling, an adorable little dragon who wasn't a shifter. He'd been found after The Fall and no one knew where he'd come from.

"I…take it you won?" Ren glanced around, looking for Hunter.

"Oh yeah." King's tone hadn't changed, but there was amusement in his ice-blue eyes. "And Hunter is currently sulking about it."

"I can't believe he actually thought he could beat me," she murmured.

"He's just a baby," Griff said, frowning.

"Oh goddess, not you too." King shook his head. "Look, he's fine. He made the challenge and he lost. It's good for him."

"I'm gonna go see him," Griff said, stepping away from them. "But I'll see you guys later."

"I swear Hunter has everyone wrapped around his little wing."

Ren lifted a shoulder, bit back a grin. "I'll probably go give him some love too. It's gotta be hard being bested in front of everyone."

Aurora and King both looked at him, shook their heads almost in unison.

"He's an adorable little menace, I swear," she muttered.

"Hey, before you head over there," King said, "I wanted to ask if you'd be up for some travel. I'd planned to talk to you tomorrow but you're here now. I know you're tight with Grace O'Connor and I'm sending her and a few others to a nearby territory that we're incorporating into our outer region. There are a bunch of humans there living on their own, and they're doing all right but they need an Alpha's protection. I need to establish the region now, before anyone comes sniffing around. I've already sent some bears in to pave the way but I need to send humans too."

"I'm in, whatever you need." He didn't even need more details. If Grace was going, he was in. "Who else is going besides me and Grace?"

"I'm not sure yet. I'm still figuring that out. But it'll be a handful of scientists. I specifically want Grace to see if she can help with any of their crops for the upcoming season. I'll probably send a witch or two. She works well with them."

Ren nodded, trying to tamp down his eagerness. No need to act like a total fool in front of his new Alpha. And that was a weird thought to have—for so long his Alpha had been a dragon female who'd up and gotten mated. Then she'd moved to her family's realm. Now he, Griff and Hyacinth had settled in New Orleans for the time being.

Though there was no "time being" for him. He was here as long as Grace was. His jaguar had claimed her even before his human side had. Like, ten whole minutes before.

He wasn't going anywhere. Even if she was dating someone else.

And soon they'd be on a mission together—he assumed without whatever asshole she was currently on a date with. Unless her date was a scientist too... Ren shelved that thought.

He'd clearly been too slow to make his move, but now that he knew she was dating again, he was done sitting on the sidelines.

CHAPTER THREE

G race frowned at the knock on her front door. She waited a moment to see if anyone else would get it. She wasn't even sure if Luna was awake—they'd stayed up late watching movies and bingeing hot chocolate. And she'd never heard Cas and Jo stir at all.

When the knock sounded again, she scooped up her mug of coffee and headed to the front door—and froze for a moment when she saw Ren through the peephole on the other side. A tall, sleek man with bronze skin and a killer smile that made her want to take all her clothes off. Yep. It was him. But…what was he doing here?

"Open the door. I know you're there, I can smell you." His tone was light, teasing.

"That is a seriously weird thing to say," Grace said as she tugged the door open.

He shrugged, his slow smile doing all sorts of things to her insides. Things she was trying to keep locked down, darn him. Why was he showing up when she was still in her pajamas, her braid likely in disarray? Oh God, had she brushed her teeth?

"Are you saying I smell bad?" she continued as she stepped back to let him in.

"Definitely not. You smell like sunshine, Grace O'Connor." He moved inside with a sort of swagger, looking around...almost curiously.

She liked the way he said her full name—and "sunshine"? That made more of those butterflies take flight inside her. What was he trying to do to her? "What's in the bag, because *it* smells delicious." She motioned for him to follow her to the kitchen.

"Muffins and pastries... Where is everyone?"

"Ah, Luna is sleeping, and..." She trailed off as her Nana stepped inside the back door to the kitchen, a small wire basket full of eggs in hand.

"Nana Josephine." Ren set down his own bag and hurried over to her, taking the basket from her and kissing the top of her head.

Her nana patted his chest gently. "Sweet boy, I'm so happy to see you this morning. What brings you by?"

"Treats," Grace said as she peered inside the bag, her stomach rumbling. Looking at the food—anything but him—was a sad attempt to avoid thinking about him and that random woman he'd been hugging, had maybe spent the night with. *Gah.*

"Well, treats and news. King was going to contact you about going on a short mission out of the territory for a few days, maybe a week. I said I'd save him the trouble."

"Mission?" She pulled down a couple plates and more mugs for them even as she shelved the disappointment that he hadn't come to see her just because.

"I don't know what else to call it. A job, I guess. Nothing dangerous," he added as he accepted the cup of coffee.

When their fingers brushed, it took all her self-control not to react to the jolt she felt straight to her core. Sweet flying dragons, just a brush of his fingers should not get her worked up.

Think, think, think—of anything other than Ren and his very capable-looking fingers, she ordered herself.

"He wants you and a couple other scientists to visit a territory he's going to be claiming. A bunch of humans living on the outskirts have been doing okay, but sooner or later a paranormal will want to claim the territory. He's doing it sooner and making sure everyone is taken care of."

"And he wants me to go?" She glanced over as her nana started breaking eggs into a bowl. She must have gotten them from one of their neighbors who had a big coop of chickens.

"Yep. Thinks you can talk with them about their crops, maybe help them if they need. There'll be some witches going too and I know you enjoy working with them."

She really did. Especially the ones who worked earth magic. Grace loved seeing science and magic work hand in hand—the reality of magic had blown open her understanding of the world around her and it was fascinating. "Obviously I'll go. You're coming too? What about Griff and Hyacinth?"

"Ah, I don't know yet. But I'm your escort."

There was something in his gaze then, something sort of heated, but no, she had to be wrong. She knew what she'd seen yesterday morning. "Sounds good. It won't take me long to pack up. When do you think we'll head out?"

"Tuesday."

She nodded, thinking of what she'd need to wrap up at work before leaving. It was Saturday so she'd have plenty of time.

"So how was your date anyway?" he asked casually before he took a sip of his coffee.

Oh, right. Her "date." *Ummmm...* She didn't want to lie, and knew he'd scent it anyway. Before she could respond, her nana turned around from the stovetop.

"Ren? I need some help reaching some of the spices. I think Cas put them up on the top shelf and we're all too short to reach them."

Whew, saved by the nana.

Ren snickered lightly and grabbed what she was asking for. "Do you need any help?"

"I do, but not in the kitchen. Grace, you go get ready. I know you haven't had a chance to shower yet, and if you hurry, you'll be able to beat the others before they wake up."

Okay that was a dismissal if she'd ever heard one...but she didn't want to worry about more dating questions so she was going to latch onto the excuse and run. "You better save me that blueberry scone though." She shot Ren a sharp look.

Which just made him grin. He put it on a separate plate and set it aside.

As she hurried out of the room, she heard the two of them start talking about gardening, which was just plain adorable.

Everything about him was adorable—and sexy. He was alpha to his bone; she'd seen him in action when he'd protected her all those months ago. But he wasn't over-the-top about it. No, the laid-back jaguar was full of charm and sweetness, and she hated that she wanted to claw out the eyes of the mystery female she'd seen him hugging. The woman was probably nice. Of course she was. Because Ren would only be with someone kind.

Damn it, she had to get out of her head. If he was dating, she'd be happy for him because they were friends. And that was what friends did.

She'd just shove down her pain as she thought of spending so much time with a male she couldn't have.

"You're going to have to step up your game if you want a chance with my granddaughter."

Ren froze at Nana Josephine's words after Grace left the room. "Pardon?"

"I believe you heard me, young man."

He was actually older than her, but he nodded. "Okay…step up my game?"

"I believe that is what the kids are saying today. And yes, because Grace won't wait around forever."

He glanced over his shoulder even though he knew Grace had gone upstairs, taking that sweet sunshine scent with her. At least she didn't smell like another male so her date must have been pretty damn boring.

Which was a good thing for the unknown male.

"You're right," he finally said.

Which earned him a surprised look from Josephine. And it quickly turned into a smile. Her auburn hair had faded, was peppered with gray, but it was easy to see the family resemblance between her and her granddaughters. Stunning, fiery females, every one of them. "It's refreshing to be told so. I want all my girls taken care of before I go. And since I'm being blunt, I want some great-grandchildren as well. They'll just be a bonus, but it would be a nice thing to give an old lady before she goes."

"Is there something I need to know about? Are you sick?"

"Don't be a smartass. And no, but you never know what could happen. I need to see my girls settled." She placed a hand over her heart. "I need that for peace."

"I'll work on the great-grandchildren thing as soon as possible, then."

She blinked at him, then grinned. "She's not going to know what hit her."

Ren grinned back and took a sip of his coffee. He knew he certainly didn't *need* the approval of Grace's grandmother or anyone, but if Josephine was telling him to go for her... Goddess, he'd been a fool to wait. He'd been holding off because of the way they'd met. She'd been attacked by her vampire date that first night and he'd saved her. She'd more or less sworn off dating so he'd been content...ish to be her friend since. But he'd always wanted more. It was impossible not to.

And if she was now dating, it was time for her to see him in a different light.

To show her that he could be everything she'd ever needed.

It was time to claim his female.

AFTER BREAKFAST, Ren hung around for a while to take care of some things around the house—including cutting down some dying branches on one of their oaks.

And as he crept along a tree branch in human form, he swore he could feel eyes on him from somewhere. Not below though.

Turning casually, he saw Grace peeking out one of the upstairs windows—her bedroom, he guessed. A room he'd never been in but had fantasized about plenty.

And she was definitely watching him. *Hmm.*

She sort of jerked when she saw him, but then waved and opened the window. "Are you being careful?" she called out.

"I'm a jaguar." He'd been climbing trees since he could run in pup form. And he was just as nimble in this form.

She frowned at him. "That's...not an answer."

He simply grinned at her and set down his axe before he stripped off his shirt.

Her eyes widened, the green sparking in the sunlight as she stared at him. Oh hell, she was definitely watching him with interest. Pure, raw, female interest.

Oooh, yes, his jaguar purred.

Just as quickly her expression went sort of neutral.

And his jaguar did not like it. "I'm being careful," he said, mainly because he wanted to reassure her. "Just don't want to get my shirt dirty."

She made a sound that wasn't a comprehensible word at all and nodded. Then after a second she shut the window and ducked out of sight but he could almost swear she was still watching him.

His jaguar wanted to preen and show off for her, but he kept his expression normal as he got to work, hacking away at the branches that were overgrown as well as the dying ones. Grace had told him which ones needed to be cut to keep the tree healthy. "I'm only doing this so you keep growing big and strong," he said to the tree because he couldn't help himself. He wasn't sure if trees or plants understood him, but he was a man who could shift into a jaguar. And he'd been in a realm before where the foliage could uproot itself. If there was ever a tree uprising in this realm, he wanted to cover his bases. "And you are a beautiful specimen of oak tree."

"You talking to the tree, Ren?"

He didn't have to look down to see Cas below. "Yep."

"Jaguars are weird."

"At least we're not lazy dragons who sleep till nine."

"I had a long night! And nine is not late."

"Uh huh. Look out," he called as he made the final hack, sending the branch falling below.

"You need some help?" Cas said a few seconds later as Ren jumped to another branch, this one higher. There were only a few strays up here he needed to trim.

"Nah, but thanks." He hoped Grace was still watching him, and he really hoped she liked what she saw. He stretched out in a patch of sunlight, enjoying the warmth before he got to work again.

"Well, well, isn't this quite the show," an unknown female voice said as he started to chop again.

Frowning, he looked down to see Cas standing with a woman he vaguely recognized. A neighbor maybe. "Back up," he called down just as Cas started herding the woman backward.

What the hell was she thinking standing under him? Rolling his eyes, he finished up, working quickly and efficiently.

"This'll make great firewood," Cas said as Ren jumped down.

"Sure will," the female said, practically licking her lips as she eyed him.

He ignored her. "Want to help me gather it? We can haul it around back to the wood pile."

"Would you mind trimming my tree?" the woman asked. "It's right across the street."

"Ah..." He started to answer as Grace strode out, an interesting expression on her face. She was smiling but it didn't reach her eyes, her lips too tight. And her stride was very determined.

"Hey Laci, how are you?" There was a sharp quality to Grace's voice as she reached them, her eyes slightly narrowed.

"Good, just hoping your friend can help out at our place. I saw him over here working and thought he might be able to help with our trees. Things have gotten kind of wild over there as you can see."

"Oh yeah, I heard your husband is out of town working on a construction project." She put a slight emphasis on the word husband. "How's he doing?"

"Great." The female's eyes narrowed slightly as she gave Grace a once-over. Then she sniffed slightly. "So can you help or not?" she asked, turning to Ren.

He lifted a shoulder. "Sure." He wasn't going to tell the woman no, even if it was clear Grace didn't like her. "Grace, you want to let me know which branches can be cut down? You're the professional."

Her expression softened as she looked at him and he didn't miss the way her gaze tracked over his chest and abs as she nodded. "Of course." And her words came out all breathy.

Yep, taking off his shirt had been a great idea. He decided to do it more often in her presence.

"You can help too, Cas," he tossed out as he picked up his axe.

The male had just been standing there, watching the exchange with a wide-eyed expression as he sipped his coffee. Ren knew Cas had grown up as a warrior, had been surrounded mostly by males or strong dragon females his entire life. He didn't always get human interactions and it was clear he found this one fascinating.

Sure enough, ten minutes later Cas murmured, "That female wants to bone you," as they reached the top branches of her oak tree.

"Did you just say 'bone'?" He eyed the overgrown foliage, tried to figure out the best approach.

"It's a word I heard Luna use the other day."

Ren snorted in amusement. "There is only one female for me."

Cas nodded. "So how was the other morning with Grace?"

He frowned at him. "What morning?"

Cas blinked, then shrugged. "Ah, I don't know. I'm confused. I'm going to start over there." Then he practically raced along the branch, heading to the opposite side of the tree, and just pounded on a branch with his fist, making it break off.

What the hell had that been about?

Ren looked down to make sure that Grace was out of range of being hurt and saw her standing with the other female on the far side of the yard. So he got to work even as he wondered at Cas's words—but more than that, he formulated a plan.

He and Grace were about to leave for a job together with no family distractions. Nothing standing between them.

It was the perfect time for him to make his move, to claim his human for good. If she'd have him. Because she might be interested physically, but he wanted more than that. He wanted all of her.

Most of all, he wanted her heart.

CHAPTER FOUR

"Are we picking up everyone else?" Grace asked as Ren loaded her bags into the back of the SUV. He'd texted her this morning to let her know he was on the way but it was the most conversation they'd had since Saturday when he'd helped out in her yard. And it was now Tuesday morning.

"Nah, change of plans." He shut the hatch and she tried so hard not to watch the flex of his muscular arms.

And failed. "Oh?"

"Yeah, just gonna be us for the drive," he said as he opened the passenger door for her.

Which was…nice, if unexpected. They weren't together or anything, and she was pretty sure he was dating. Or at least sleeping with someone. And that thought sent a splash of ice-cold water across her face. *Ugh.* But…wait… "Just the two of us?"

He grinned as he shut the door and rounded the front of the vehicle.

Just the two of them on a road trip. Ooooh, she wasn't sure how she was going to deal with that. She'd been ready to claw off her neighbor's face on Saturday for trying to flirt with Ren. The woman was married but Grace knew she wasn't faithful to her husband. And she thought she could come on to Ren?

"What's that look? I'm great on road trips, despite what my crew might have told you," he said as he started the vehicle.

She knew this SUV was spelled so they didn't have to worry about gas—in this territory witches had been working to spell necessary items. And while supernaturals could often get to places easily enough with speed, it wasn't the same for humans. Not to mention unless you were a dragon it was also difficult to transport much without vehicles.

"Why would your crew have told me anything different?" He had to be referring to Hyacinth or Griffin. Or potentially Juniper, but she lived in another realm now with her family and new mate.

"Ah, no reason. Never mind."

"You can't get away with that," she said as she twisted back and opened the cooler wedged between the back seat bench and the front. "Oh, so much fresh fruit, yum. Where'd you get all this?"

"One of King's wolves packed it—because if I'm being honest, I'd have packed gummy worms and Fritos."

She let out a startled burst of laughter. "Seriously?"

"Yep. Fine palate right here." He gave her a wicked grin and she felt that look down deep.

Sooooo deep. Whew. She was glad when he looked back at the road and focused on driving. Because if he was looking away from her, she could actually think straight. "This is a new side to you."

He lifted a shoulder, shot her a quick glance. "I have many sides you haven't seen yet." It almost sounded as if there was a sensual edge to his tone.

She...did not know how to respond to that. She cleared her throat, glanced out the window. "So, tell me what the plan is. How long it should take to get there, whatever I need to know."

"Didn't King send you the info?"

Guiltily she peeked a glance at him. "Yeah, but I got busy with wrapping up some stuff yesterday then crashed hard. I only woke up a couple hours ago and had just enough time to pack before you got here."

"It's not like I would have left you if you hadn't."

She laughed lightly. "So yeah, I didn't read much, just scanned the info. We're headed to an outer ring of the territory basically."

"Yep. There's a decent enough road to get us there too. The others actually flew by dragon and were able to leave early so that's why it's just the two of us."

He seemed intent on reminding her of that as they headed out of the city, jumping onto the highway, which had only a couple vehicles going in either direction. In the before times, I-10 would have been jam-packed with stop-and-go traffic until they got out of the city proper. And even then it would have still been crowded, just not so crammed. This…was different.

"It's weird being out here," she murmured, looking at the various construction sites and big garden spaces they passed on the highway.

"Oh, right. Have you been outside the city at all since The Fall?"

"No." And right now a weird sensation settled in her gut… Maybe fear of venturing into the unknown. She knew they were still in King's territory, but this made her feel almost unsafe. She hadn't even thought about that when she'd agreed to leave.

"Hey." Ren's voice was low, concerned, and she nearly jumped when she felt his hand on her knee. "You okay?"

"Yeah." She tried to keep her voice light as she turned back to him. "Just setting in that I'm leaving my family and everyone I know. I mean, I know we're not going too far, and before everything I wouldn't have blinked at traveling. It's not like the world was any safer then but I sure believed the illusion that it was."

"I'm with you." His jaguar flashed in his gaze. "I'll keep you safe. No matter what."

She breathed out a sigh, nodded, because she trusted him. Had trusted him from practically the moment they'd met. Well, maybe not then because she hadn't really noticed him. But when she'd been attacked by that vampire she'd gone on a date with, Ren had saved her. And he'd been her friend ever since.

She swallowed hard. Even if she couldn't have more with him, she cherished his friendship. And him. "Thank you." She took his hand in hers and squeezed.

Then she let it go almost immediately because if he was taken by someone else, she didn't want to overstep her bounds.

He looked as if he wanted to say more, but then cleared his throat, pulled out a CD holder. "You get to pick the music."

"I'm glad you still have CDs," she murmured, thumbing through his music, not surprised that his taste in music spanned decades. Often she forgot how old he was because he acted like such a goofball at times.

"Of course… And for the record I have gummy bears if you decide you want some."

She snickered even as she pulled a disc out. "I feel so honored you'll share them with me."

"I'd share anything and everything with you." His tone was uncharacteristically serious.

And she did not know how to take it or his words. So she slid the disc into the player and turned up the music. Was she just imagining the vibe between them? Projecting?

Leaning her head back against the headrest, she closed her eyes as the rock song played. She needed to keep it together or else she'd do something really stupid on this drive. Like confess her feelings to him.

A LOUD POP sounded and Ren gripped the wheel of the SUV tight.

"What was that?" Grace straightened in her seat, pretty sure she already knew the answer to her question.

"What it sounds like, unfortunately," Ren growled as he pulled over onto the side of the road.

Not that it really mattered since they were on a back country two-lane road with fields on either side of them. They hadn't stayed on the highway too long, had instead gotten off and headed north.

"It'll be fine. There should be a spare."

But…there wasn't.

Grace eyed Ren, who looked more frustrated than she'd ever seen him. King's wolf pack had given them an SUV to take and they'd both assumed it would be in good shape. "So…what do we do?" They were two hours' driving time from where they were supposed to be, but that was a crazy long walk. Not to mention they wouldn't be able to haul all their supplies with them anyway.

"Since I can't hunt down the wolf who forgot to make sure there was a spare tire in the vehicle...I'm going to call Griff, see if he can run one up here to us."

Grace glanced around, struck by how overgrown and green everything was. Birds chirped happily and she could see a couple farmhouses in the distance. But no real signs of human life. This sort of felt like the start to a horror movie: broken down on the side of the road with—

"Hey, it's gonna be fine," Ren said, drawing her attention to him as he held his phone to his ear. He really did read her well, or maybe he just scented her distress. "Griff, it's me," he said, taking a step away.

Get it together, Grace, she silently ordered herself. At home she was so used to pivoting and just dealing with various work crises. This just felt scarier, out here in the wild territory where so many things were unknown.

She started putting the bags in the back as Ren talked. He'd pulled everything out, popped open the cover to the spare, only to find it empty. Then he'd let out a colorful curse. At least he was so steady about everything.

Which made her feel steady. And a little silly, if she was being honest. She was with a hot male who could turn into a deadly jaguar. She'd be all right. They both would.

"Hey, leave that," Ren said as he suddenly stepped around the back of the vehicle. "I'll put them back."

"I can lift my own bags."

He made a sort of grunting sound of disagreement that shouldn't be so adorable. "We're going to have to wait for a while so let's just grab a few essentials for now."

"A while?"

"Yeah, Griff's gonna head this way soon, but he's tying up something so it'll be a bit. We can explore a little if you want? I want to check out those houses. And I scent a source of water nearby. A river or stream. No people though. You want to explore?"

"Sure," she said and realized she did. She wanted to get a lay of the land, and since she was outside New Orleans, she needed to take advantage. The old Grace had loved traveling and she missed it. "Let's grab some snacks and waters and do this."

He gave her a quick grin as he pulled out his backpack and started prepping.

She was going to look at this from a positive side—at least she got to spend more time with Ren, just the two of them. Even if they were destined to only be friends.

CHAPTER FIVE

"We could just sleep in the SUV." Grace stood in front of the long-abandoned farmhouse as Ren stepped outside the house he'd just gone inside to scope out.

Darkness was about to fall and Griff still wasn't here. He was supposed to have shown up hours ago. They'd done some exploring of the area and it was clear that anyone who'd lived here had moved elsewhere. Other than some free-roaming cows and horses, they hadn't seen anything else. It had been weirdly nice to hike along the stream, if strange to be the only two people out here.

"Nah, this place is fine. Dusty, but fine. Whoever lived here packed up and left a while ago so it's doubtful anyone is going to surprise us."

She eyed the house, glancing around as cicadas started up in the trees. They sounded so loud out here.

"I've already set up a room for you."

"Uh, we're not sleeping in separate rooms," she snapped out as she turned back around. "If that's what you're thinking."

He blinked once. "Ah, no."

But it was clear he'd thought she'd sleep alone. *Oh, hell no.* That was like the start to a horror movie. *Nope.* "Let's just roll out our sleeping bags in the same room," she said as she hurried up the steps. It was getting too dark and she was suddenly feeling like a big ole chicken. This was a very different kind of dark than in the city. There weren't any ambient lights or street lights or…anything. Just their solar-powered lanterns and some candles Ren had found.

"Living room is probably the best place, then," he said as he moved inside with her.

She could see immediately that he was right. There was a sense of stillness as she stepped inside. And dust coated the flat surfaces that she could see.

"We could sleep out under the stars," Ren said behind her, making her jump.

"Seriously?"

He shrugged. "I sleep in my jaguar form more often than not."

For a moment, she wondered… Whew, she wondered a *lot* about his sleeping habits, but she wasn't letting her mind wander in that direction. She turned around, stepped into the living room. "Maybe when we get back to New Orleans I'll take you up on sleeping out under the stars." She'd be too nervous to sleep out here, even with Ren next to her. Intellectually she knew the walls of the house wouldn't protect her, but it was a visual thing she needed to feel safe. And at home it would be different.

"I'm going to hold you to that," he murmured as he moved the couch and coffee table away from the fireplace to create a bigger space. "Want me to start a fire?"

"Yes, please. I can help you gather firewood."

He shot her a look she couldn't decipher. "How about you just set up our sleeping bags and I'll grab the wood?"

"It kinda feels like you're trying hard not to order me to stay put."

His answering grin held a hint of wicked—and he didn't respond as he hurried out the front door.

Her stomach was in wild knots as he left because of that smile—and simply because of him. They were going to be sleeping next to each other. Alone. In the middle of nowhere. "And I need to get it together," she ordered herself for like the billionth time.

Ignoring the butterflies inside her at the prospect of the coming night, she started setting up their bedrolls. Then she dusted a bit around where they'd be sleeping and set up candles next to the glowing lantern. They'd do until they got the fireplace going.

Once everything was set up, she looked at some of the dusty, framed photographs on the mantel and sideboard. From the photos, she gathered that this place had belonged to an older couple, closer to her nana's age, and they'd had a lot of kids and grandkids in the pictures.

She could see what Ren had meant about them packing up after she'd explored the house with the lantern. Everything was neat and tidy, but they'd emptied out the fridge and garbage so there were no smells, and most of the clothing and a handful of frames had clearly been taken.

She hoped they were now living with family, safe somewhere. Her own parents hadn't made it and... She swallowed down the surge of emotion, then paused when she heard a sound from downstairs.

"Grace?"

Her heart rate kicked up at the sound of Ren's delicious voice. "I'm here."

She plucked up the lantern and hurried downstairs to find him lugging in a handful of wood and what she and her sisters called "lighter." When pine trees died, the sap moved to the middle of the tree and hardened—and burned hot. Hence the term lighter. It was perfect kindling, something Ren apparently knew. Because of course he did. The male was so in touch with nature and the world around them.

And he was totally shirtless again. All cut lines and striations—he was ridiculously sculpted. Was he trying to kill her? "Need any help?"

"I got it. Thanks for setting up our beds."

Okay she was definitely imagining the sensual way he said "our beds." *Right?*

"Did you hear from Griff?" she asked as she sat across from him, catty-corner to the fireplace, and tried not to stare as he got the fire going. As the shadows from the licking flames played off his perfect pecs.

Oh sweet heavens, this was too much. And she was going to be sleeping beside him tonight.

"Yeah, finally. He's running really late so it's a good thing we're setting up here. I gave him directions, but he'll smell the fire anyway."

She nodded, feeling kind of useless even as exhaustion started creeping in. They'd done a lot of hiking today as they'd checked out the area.

"You mind if I sleep without my shirt on?" Ren asked into the quiet crackling of the wood.

"What?"

He patted his flat, washboard abs almost absently. "I run hotter and normally don't sleep in anything. But if it makes you uncomfortable, I'll put my shirt back on."

"Oh, no." Dang it, why did her voice have to come out all breathy? "Ah, it's fine. Sleep however you want. Are you...tired now?"

"A little. How about you?"

"I'm pretty tired." But also keyed up now that he was running around shirtless. Something was seriously wrong with her.

"Let's catch some sleep, then," he said as he started unzipping his sleeping bag at the top.

She slipped her cardigan off, then pulled her bra off without taking her shirt off—which made him blink. "What?"

His mouth curved up, and once again he gave her an unreadable look. "Nothing."

"That look was something," she murmured as she got into her own sleeping bag.

"I was just impressed with that move, but then thought I probably shouldn't comment on your bra."

She simply laughed and stretched out. "We're friends, it's fine." She would give almost anything to be more though.

He gave her a dark look then, but it was gone quickly as he stretched out next to her, letting out a little sigh as he did.

And man, he smelled so good. Like the forest, all wild and masculine, and it took all her self-control not to roll over and just bury her face against his chest. Because yeah, that was so not what friends did.

"What was your favorite part about today?" she asked a few minutes later into the semi-quiet. The fire created a decent amount of white noise, easing some of her anxiety.

"Besides hanging out with you, just being in nature was my favorite. Getting to stretch my legs."

Um, besides hanging out with her? He just said that. What was he trying to do to her? Why did he have to be so damn perfect?

"What about you?" he murmured.

"Hanging out with you," she said, then wondered if that was too weird for a friend to say.

He was silent for a long moment, the tension between them seeming to stretch until he said, "So, you never said how your date was."

Ooooh. Right. Craaaap. She'd forgotten about that. "No, I didn't," she said on a laugh because she didn't like lying. "So who are you dating?" If he was going to open this up, she was getting answers. Something deep inside her, some compulsion wanted to know about that mystery woman she'd seen him hugging.

"No one."

She snorted before she could stop herself.

"Hey," he growled, turning toward her.

So she did the same, curling on her side, using her arm to prop her head up as she watched him.

His dark eyes had the faintest slivers of amber circling his irises as he watched her. "You don't believe me?"

"I..." Okay, she wasn't going to admit she'd gone to his place because then he'd want to know why. And she couldn't tell him another lie. Sure, she hadn't actually told him she'd gone on a date, her sister had. But he thought it had come from her and she'd never corrected him. So, yeah. "It's just hard to believe, that's all."

"Why?"

Now she snorted intentionally. "Oh come on, I know you have a mirror."

He blinked, then a slow grin spread across his far too handsome face. "Are you saying I'm attractive?"

"I'm not feeding your ego," she grumbled as she turned onto her back, stared up at the white ceiling. The fan was still, of course, and she focused on the two pulls hanging down from it.

"Well, I'm not dating. Anyone. And why won't you tell me about your date? I thought you'd sworn off men."

"I didn't swear off men." Frowning, she turned on her side to face him again. He was still watching her carefully, which should have been unnerving. And okay, it kind of was. But she liked it when he watched her, wanted to bask under his dark gaze.

"Yeah you did. After what happened with that vampire," he said on a growl, his jaguar peering back at her.

"Oh..." She laughed lightly. "Right. I was just mad. And scared, but I didn't swear off dating or anything."

He blinked, his eyes human again. "I thought..." He cleared his throat, reached out a hand, then froze, his head tilting slightly before he shoved up. "Stay put," he ordered, then bolted out the front door.

CHAPTER SIX

R en stepped into the foyer. "Gra—" He ducked as she jumped out from behind the door, fire poker in hand. "It's just me and Griff!"

"Oh my God," she breathed out, setting the poker against the wall as Griff stepped in with him. "I couldn't see anything when I peeked out the windows."

"Hey, short stuff," Griff said as he pulled her into a big hug. "Glad you didn't clock me in the head."

As Griff hugged her, Ren had to remind himself that Griff was his oldest friend. His best friend. A male he loved like a brother. Not a male he now wanted to murder and rip off his face for daring to touch Grace. "All right, that's enough," he growled, his jaguar right at the surface.

"Wait...what?" Grace frowned at him as she stepped back, clearly confused.

"Griff is late and we need to change the tire." It was pathetic as far as excuses went but whatever. He was telling her the truth—that he didn't want any male touching her. Ever.

"Nah, we can do it in the morning. It's too dark." Griff slung an arm around her shoulders and gave Ren a mischievous grin. "Ren's just grumpy. Cats get like that if their sleep gets interrupted."

Yeah, well, they hadn't been sleeping. And he swore they'd had a moment. And he'd been about to make a move. A long overdue one. Until an asshole had interrupted them.

Ren shoved Griff's arm off her shoulders then grabbed him in a headlock. Grace let out a yelp even as Griff laughed and punched him in the stomach.

"Oh my God," she breathed. "You're worse than the dragon brothers."

He was aware of her moving back out of the way as they fell to the ground and then rolled out the front door. He knew he was being a psycho but this was what shifters did. And Griff shouldn't have touched her.

His friend had been intentionally screwing with him. Now he was going to pay.

"Been a while since we tussled," Griff muttered.

"Been a while since I broke your fucking nose too," he growled, headbutting Griff.

"Damn it, Ren!" Griff held up his hands and stood in the front yard, the moonlight and stars their only illumination as blood streamed down his face. "I was just messing with you." He glanced back to the house where no doubt Grace was watching them. "I didn't realize you were so edgy."

"Well I am." His jaguar was right under the surface, desperate and needy for Grace. His mate. He could sense it in a way he'd never experienced, never actually understood. Not until he'd met her.

"I'm sorry." Griff held out a hand and Ren clasped his arm as Griff clasped his.

"Apology accepted."

"Are you guys good?" Grace called out from the porch.

"Yeah. I deserved it," Griff said before Ren could respond, and started cleaning the blood off his face. "I ate all his peanut butter and he's still pissed."

Grace just snorted and muttered something about weird shifter habits and headed back inside.

"Peanut butter?"

"It was all I could think of. Unless you want me to tell her the truth?"

Ren cuffed him on the shoulder before he raced inside, found Grace straightening out their sleeping bags. "Sorry about that."

She just let out a light laugh. "Cas and his brothers are way worse. It's eye-opening how violent shifters get with each other, then act as if everything's fine. I'm just gonna roll with it."

"So you, Luna, and Jo never fight?" he asked as he added another log to the fire.

"I didn't say that. We're just much, much sneakier about things. And we don't punch each other."

"Sounds like Hyacinth," Griff said as he came into the room, dropped his pack by the couch and pulled out his own sleeping bag. "She'll shave off your hair in the middle of the night if you piss her off." He ran his hand over his dark hair, likely reliving the time she'd done just that.

"Um...we're not that sneaky. I think my sisters would actually kill me if I touched their hair. And vice versa." She ran her hand over her auburn braid, mock shuddered.

Ren reached out and ran his fingers down her long braid, gently tugged it. "I love your hair."

A sweet scent rolled off her, and even in the dimness he could see the flush of her cheeks thanks to the fire. "Thanks... So, I guess we're all just sleeping here? Griff, are you hungry or should we all crash?"

"I ate before I got here. I'm good."

Ren took over then. "You sleep closest to the fire," he murmured to Grace. "You need the warmth more than us. Then he cut Griff a sharp look because Ren would be the one sleeping next to her.

Griff simply shook his head and stretched out on his backpack, not bothering to change or strip. The only thing he took off were his shoes before the wolf basically dropped into a dead sleep.

"Is he really sleeping?" Grace peered over at Griff as she stretched out too.

"Yeah, wolves are like that. Can just sleep anywhere."

"I'm impressed," she said around a yawn.

"Here," he said, wrapping his arm around her. "You can use me for warmth too."

To his surprise, she curled right into him. "You're warmer than the fire."

Yep, warm her up good, his jaguar ordered. *Please her all night.*

Like he was going to do anything with Griff mere feet away? *Don't be a jackass*, he growled at his beast half.

His jaguar simply sniffed haughtily at him.

He ordered his heart rate to slow down as he wrapped his arm tighter around Grace and held her close. She fit against him perfectly, as if she'd been made for him.

REN BIT back a growl as Grace snuggled even more against him, her face now buried in his neck as she soaked up his warmth.

He'd been awake for the last hour because his body had simply woken up at the feel of Grace plastered against him. He knew she was cold, and he would have restarted the fire but that would have meant moving. And the sun had just risen. They wouldn't be staying much longer, so no sense in starting another fire.

So he let her take his warmth, and he enjoyed feeling her wrapped around him. She'd thrown one leg over him, had her face against his neck and was holding him like he was her favorite plushie. And since he'd opted to sleep without a shirt, she'd been rubbing her hand over his chest on and off for the last hour. It was heaven and hell.

Of course Griff was still snoozing; the wolf could sleep through a tornado.

Inhaling, Ren tried not to feel like too much of a perv as he drank in her sweet sunshine lavender scent.

Then she made a sort of groaning sound and raised her head, blinked those gorgeous green eyes at him. "Ren?" She blinked again, glanced around. "You're warm," she murmured sleepily and dropped her head back on him, snuggling against him.

Then she froze, and he could feel the moment she started to pull away so he tightened his grip on her. "I like having you cuddled up against me." He kept his voice pitched low.

She stopped breathing for a moment, but then her body melded against his again. Though she was still a little tense. "Did you sleep okay?"

"Yep. You're the best cuddle buddy." Was he laying it on too thick? Being a weirdo?

She stiffened again. "Do you have a lot of *cuddle* buddies?" Her face was still buried against him, more on his chest now.

Griff sat up then, yawned loudly as he looked at the two of them. "Morning, guys. Ya'll ready to head out soon?"

Ren wanted to punch his best friend.

Grace pushed up without looking at Ren and murmured something about "taking care of personal business" before she hurried out of the room. Moments later he heard the back door open then close.

As he sat up, Ren shoved his hands through his hair, wanted to pull it all out in frustration. "Hell, Griff. You sleep through actual demon attacks but you decide to wake up now. You are the king of shitty timing."

"What did I do?"

"Nothing," he muttered, all the muscles in his body tense. He couldn't believe Grace had actually asked if he had a lot of cuddle buddies.

"Sorry, brother." Griff shoved to his feet, yawned and stretched.

"One day I hope to repay the favor."

"Hey, mean!" But Griff had a smile on his face as he hurried out the front door, likely to take care of "personal business" too.

Ren started packing up his and Grace's things, but he couldn't pack up his feelings. Couldn't keep them locked down anymore. Not well anyway.

This morning had made that pretty clear.

CHAPTER SEVEN

"I heard through the grapevine you're dating someone, Griff," Grace said before popping a grape in her mouth.

Ren forced himself not to look over at her from the driver's seat. He needed to focus on the road, not her, or he was going to get them all into a crash. They'd quickly packed up the SUV, changed the tire, then headed out, leaving Griff's vehicle hidden away near the farmhouse. Not that they were really worried about anyone taking it.

"Who'd you hear that from?" Griff asked from the back.

"I have my ways." She turned around and tossed a grape at Griff.

"Well you heard wrong," his best friend said.

"Hmm. I don't know if I buy it."

"Speaking of dating, how was your date the other night?" Ren asked in what he hoped was a casual tone. This was the perfect transition since he'd never gotten his question answered the other day. Almost as if she was trying to avoid the topic.

"Oh..." Grace cleared her throat.

"Yeah, turnabout's fair play," Griff added. "Spill it."

"There was no date," she murmured. The scent rolling off her was... off somehow. He couldn't put his finger on it.

And the relief that punched through Ren was so potent, he nearly tore the steering wheel off.

"Why not?" Griff asked and Ren wanted to hug him. Suddenly felt bad for making him bleed last night.

Because he couldn't be the one to ask all the questions, even if he wanted to know everything about that fucking date—that thankfully hadn't happened.

"Oh my God, nosy!" Grace threw another grape at him. "And none of your business. There was no date, so it doesn't matter. What about you, Ren? Who are you dating?"

Griff howled in the back. "He's not dating anyone."

Ren glanced at Grace. "He's not wrong." He'd also told her the same last night but apparently she didn't believe him.

"You're really not?" She seemed truly surprised by his words.

"Nope."

A curious smile curved her lips, but then she changed the topic and said, "So Griff, I want to hear road trip stories about Ren."

And that launched his best friend into telling embarrassing stories about him—which was fine with Ren.

Grace hadn't gone on a date with anyone. And she seemed truly surprised but happy that he wasn't dating anyone.

He seriously needed to have a private conversation with her—to make it clear he didn't want anyone but her.

"GRACE!" a booming male voice called out, making Ren and Griff turn from the open hatch of the SUV.

They'd parked along Main Street—that was actually the name of the street—in the small town that had clearly kept things running smoothly since The Fall. All the shops had clean windows, though he doubted the town looked the way it would have before The Fall. No signs advertising things for sale, but he could see fresh food on display through one window and what looked like crocheted clothing and blankets through another. And there was dried meat visible through a window across the street.

They'd been waved in by a couple bears at the entrance to the town —definitely security—and told to park and someone would come get them. Now it seemed someone had. And Ren found himself annoyed that Grace's smile was so huge for Logan—a bear shifter he genuinely liked—who was approaching them.

"Logan, I didn't know you were here," Grace said as the giant male swooped in and picked her up off her feet in a hug.

Ren's jaguar swiped at him until Logan put her down—then did the same thing to Ren.

"Ren!" Then Logan hugged Griff, patting him hard on the back. "I've missed all of you!"

Ren found himself laughing at the Alpha bear who was impossible not to like. "I saw you a week ago down at Cynara's club."

Logan lifted a broad shoulder—the male had to be over six feet five because Ren was well over six feet. "Still, it's nice to see familiar faces. My bears have started integrating with the humans, but it's not the same as New Orleans. And I'm sorry to say we only have one room left." He winced slightly as he looked between the three of them.

"Grace and I can share," Ren said before Griff could say a word.

Thankfully his best friend said, "I can pitch a tent or just bunk up with some of your bears."

"Is this acceptable to you?" Logan asked Grace.

"Yeah, of course. We'll make anything work. We're here to help out and I know we're late, so if you want to point me in the right direction I'm ready to get to it. Right?"

She looked at Griff and Ren, and Ren desperately wished he had the right to call her his, to kiss her before they separated.

"That's the attitude I like. Okay, I'll have someone take all your stuff to the room and..." Logan nodded to someone in the distance, waved over a petite, dark-haired, bronze-skinned female who smelled human. "Koa, this is Ren and Griff, and the lovely Grace. She'll be working with your crew."

"It's nice to meet you…" Grace looked at Ren and Griff and smiled. "I'll see you guys later, I guess?"

"I won't take them too far, I promise," Logan said with a gentle clap on her shoulder before the human and Grace strode off.

Ren watched her go, shoved down the primal urge to stalk after her, kiss her senseless and let her and everyone else watching know that she belonged to him.

"She's not leaving the territory," Logan said, misreading Ren's expression. "She'll stick with the humans and witches and probably help them with the crops and greenhouses. You two, however," he said, now lowering his booming voice, "I'm glad you're here."

"What's up?" Ren immediately went into soldier mode, as Juniper used to say. "Do I need my arrows?" He had magical arrows he used in battle, though since settling in New Orleans he didn't always bring them with him on territory patrols.

"I don't think so. Not now. I just want to give you two a lay of the land and perimeter. We've had some weird stuff happening—before we got here thankfully, so the humans don't suspect us. But food has been missing. It's random, and once I show you around," he said, motioning with a sweep of his hand, "you'll see that there's no need to steal. The people here have set up an incredible system, much similar to the one in our territory. Anyone can take what they need. But entire trees will have their apples go missing overnight. And there have been no odd scents anyone can pick up."

"What about tracks?" Ren asked.

"Nothing." Logan frowned, then waved at someone across the street. "But I know you two are excellent trackers."

"Griff more than me," Ren said, because it was true. "He's like a ghost."

"Don't let his humble attitude fool you. The feline is sneaky too. Just show us where food's been taken and we can sniff around," Griff said.

Ren nodded his agreement, ready to get to work. Otherwise he'd obsess over where Grace was right now. And who she was with.

Tonight he was going to talk to her about him—them. Tell her how he felt.

CHAPTER EIGHT

"I had fun with you today," Koa said to Grace as they reached the communal eating area.

A bunch of picnic tables were set up on what had once been a field of some type. Maybe baseball. She could see faint white lines on the ground but now there were solar lights strung up everywhere and a couple food trucks that seemed to be a permanent thing.

"Thanks, I had fun too. I'm so impressed with how much you guys have kept things running. Being in a city with a good Alpha has made such a difference. It's easy to forget that not everyone has that."

Koa nodded, her expression introspective as they got in line at one of the food trucks. "It's weird how quickly we've all started using the word Alpha here."

"So...you guys are okay accepting King as your Alpha?" She'd wanted to ask when she'd been working in the greenhouses today with Koa, but it had felt like too much for a first conversation. They'd been pretty focused on working with different hybrid crops anyway, one of her favorite things to do.

"At first I had reservations, but King was really smart sending the bears in," Koa said on a laugh. "Either they're the best actors in the world and they're running a long con or..." She shook her head, laughing. "They're amazing. And I know they're not lying. We were doing okay on our own but the world is different now. And even though it sucks, it's reality that another pack or whatever could come in and take our territory by force. It's really nice not to have to worry about that."

"King is a very smart Alpha," Grace said. "Everyone loves the bears."

"So what's it like in the city? I've been to New Orleans before but just on vacations. Are things really different now?"

"Yeah. A lot's the same but a lot is different. In a good way though." Grace was aware of a couple people in front of them in line having turned slightly to listen.

So she smiled at the two women who she guessed were humans.

Koa nudged one. "Quit being nosy."

The female with blonde hair wearing overalls and a flannel shirt over them said, "Kinda hard not to overhear. So yeah, what's the city like now?"

"First," Koa said, "Grace, this is Ellen, and Salma," she said, nodding at the other woman, who'd been quiet.

After introductions were made, Grace said, "Difference mainly is that you can be walking down the street, or bike riding in my case, and see a full-grown lion just strutting down the street."

Salma grinned. "Seriously?"

"Yep. And if there's like a big party or something, I've seen so many shifters play sports in their animal form—wearing crazy stuff like tutus."

That got her laughter and more questions.

So she explained how King had basically revitalized the territory, making sure there was enough housing, food and healthcare for everyone, as well as working to basically "hurricane proof" the city by working with witches and other supernaturals.

By the time they made it to the front of the line, Koa's bronze cheeks had flushed as she greeted the female running the food truck. "Hey, Estrid."

"Hey Koa. I already made you a plate." The female's smile was just as wide as Koa's as they sort of stared at each other.

"Thanks...ah, this is Grace. We've been working together today."

Grace smiled at the female—got a curt nod and a plate full of fresh fruit and a grilled cheese shoved at her. *All right, then.* Grace bit back a smile as Koa picked up her plate and she did the same and headed over to a table.

"So...that your girlfriend?" Grace vaguely recognized the tall, sleek blonde who looked as if she could have stepped off a Viking ship. She was a bear shifter from New Orleans.

"What?" Koa shook her head as she motioned toward an empty bench and table. "No. We're just friends."

Grace surreptitiously glanced at the food piled on Koa's plate versus her own. Her plate was fine, but Koa's looked like a Christmas dinner kind of plate—a little bit of everything was on it. "Yeah, I've got a friend like that too," she murmured. One she wanted to be more with.

Koa blinked, then laughed as they sat.

Before they'd touched their plates, Ren and Griff seemingly appeared out of nowhere, sitting on either side of her.

"Hey guys," she said as she popped some pineapple in her mouth. She liked Ren so close to her, felt as if maybe something had shifted between them. He'd told her that he really was single and Griff had backed it up.

"Hey yourself." Ren nudged her shoulder with his, his grin all charming and wicked.

And for the billionth time, she wondered what it would be like to kiss him, get naked with him...do all the things with him.

They all started talking, Koa just as friendly with them as she'd been with Grace. And before she knew it, she'd polished off everything on her plate and was still kinda hungry, which surprised her. But maybe it shouldn't, because she'd only eaten some nuts and a protein bar for lunch.

"Here," Koa said, maybe reading her mind or expression as she passed her plate to the middle of the table. "This is way too much food. You guys are all free to take what you want."

Griff's hand reached out lightning fast but Ren reached over Grace and smacked him. "Let her pick first, savage."

She just snickered and snagged the chocolate brownie. That should hit her sweet tooth right. "Thanks, Koa."

"So what happens around here at night?" Griff asked Koa even as Logan approached their table.

The big bear nodded at everyone politely, then said, "Grace, you got a sec?"

"Ah, yeah, of course." She shot Ren a curious look, wondering if he knew what this was about, but he just frowned at Logan.

Huh. Okay, then. She grabbed her brownie, not trusting Griff not to eat it as she joined Logan. "What's up?"

"Walk with me, okay?"

"Is everything all right?" she murmured as they headed across the big field toward a group of homes. And she swore she could feel Ren's gaze on her, but didn't want to look like a weirdo and check.

He rubbed a hand over his dark hair, seeming nervous. "Yeah, I... need you to take something back to New Orleans for me. A gift. For Zia."

Oooh, right. Grace had heard that Logan had a thing for Zia—who ran one of the largest construction crews in New Orleans right now. "Are you guys together now?"

He lifted a big shoulder as they reached a small cabin, one of many surrounded by others that looked fairly new. "Not yet, but we will be. Wait here?"

She nodded as he hurried inside, then moments later he came out with a small brown package.

He placed it carefully in her hands. "There are many letters in there for her. And..." He held out another package, slightly opened it for Grace to see.

She blinked. "Is that a carving of you?"

He nodded, dead serious. "Of course. She needs something to remember me."

"I don't think she could forget you."

Logan gave her a huge smile. "That's what I tell myself too, but she's a stubborn human. Ah...not that I think all humans are stubborn."

Grace shrugged. "My family is full of stubborn females so no offense taken."

His shoulders relaxed. "I trust you to take all this back to her, and I think it would be better if a human brings her these things and not one of my clanmates. They're too nosy."

"Of course. I'll keep this with my things, and when I return I'll make sure she gets everything. I promise."

He shoved out a sigh, as if he'd actually been worried she'd say no. Logan was one of the Alphas of the territory—he ran a huge clan of bears along with another bear—but it was clear he'd fallen hard for the human. Grace liked him so she hoped Zia returned his feelings.

"You're a good human, Grace," he said as he started back toward the dining area. "So, tell me about your first day."

"I will if you show me where my room is." The one she'd be sharing with Ren. "I'd like to put this up and see where I'll be sleeping tonight."

Lies. She desperately wanted to see what the bed situation was. Was it one bed? She sure hoped so.

CHAPTER NINE

Ren watched as Logan and Grace headed off toward where the bear housing was, and now they were headed in another direction.

"You've gotta ease back on the aggression," Griff murmured to Ren as he got up, started to follow after Grace and Logan.

Stupid, good-looking bear. "What?" Blinking, he glanced at Griff, saw that Koa had left. Crap, had he even said goodbye to her?

"The waves of aggression rolling off you are a lot. Ease up."

Hell. "You're right, I'm gonna go take a walk. See ya later." He stood, moved quickly before Griff could respond, and headed in the same direction as Grace and Logan.

They were about a hundred yards in front of him and disappeared past a group of cabins. The bear was probably just showing her to their room, but Ren didn't like her out of his sight.

Not when he'd been separated from her all day, and especially not now that the sun had set.

It didn't take him long to make it to the three-story brick building in the small downtown area. Grace's scent was strong as he hurried up the stairs to the third floor, where their room was.

Their. Room.

Yeah, he liked the sound of that.

Thankfully he didn't scent Logan as he reached their door. His jaguar was too close to the surface to deal with the bear.

Using his key, he opened the door, heard water running. Then a moment later Grace stepped out of the bathroom. She blinked, then smiled when she saw him and it was like the damn sun came out from behind the clouds.

Yeah, he was gone. Just utterly gone over her.

"Hey," she said, smiling as she glanced at their packed bags. "I so don't want to deal with unpacking our stuff."

He didn't either, unless he got to unpack her. Or would it be unwrap her? Yeah, unwrap. "So let's don't. Want to go for a walk? I got to explore some of the outer territory today and there are some nice lakes and streams." And if they happened to get naked and go swimming, even better.

"I'm in—but I'm calling first shower when we get back." Her grin was mischievous as she said it.

Or they could shower together. Save water. He kept that thought to himself, however. "Deal."

It didn't take long for Ren to lead her to one of the places he'd seen earlier in the day. A secluded lake surrounded by woods—and no people around for miles.

"Okay, this place is gorgeous." Awe tinged Grace's voice as they reached the edge of the lake twenty minutes later. There were no lights this far from the small township, but the moon and stars were brilliant tonight.

"A natural spring feeds it so it's an even temperature all year round too," he said as he slipped off his boots. Then his shirt.

"What are you doing?" Her eyes were wide as she watched him.

"What's it look like?" he asked as he shucked his pants.

She let out a yelp of surprise and turned around. "Ah, getting naked for some inexplicable reason?"

"It's time for a swim."

"You're serious," she murmured, and when he turned he saw her peeking over her shoulder.

He grinned—and she turned back around.

"What about gators?" she called out.

"It's too cold here, the wolves already told me. Besides, I can easily handle a gator."

"That is such a weird thing to say… Turn around!"

Oh hell yeah. If she was telling him to turn around, she was getting in.

"I've turned," he called out as he waded into the water, savored the chill of it. He hadn't been lying about running hotter. As a jaguar, his blood naturally ran warmer than a human, and despite what people thought about felines, he loved the water.

At the sound of water moving behind him, his entire body tensed, all his muscles going taut. She was actually getting in with him. Maybe naked.

"Can't believe I let you talk me into this," she grumbled.

"I didn't even have to convince you," he started, but froze as he turned and saw she was definitely naked. Not even in her bra and underwear, but completely, gloriously naked.

Grace's lower half was under the water and she was now up to her waist and had her arm across her full breasts but…still, a naked Grace. It took a moment for his brain to process that she was only a few feet away, *with no clothes on.*

Fuck. Yeah.

"What?" she demanded.

He cleared his throat. "Just thinking you look good in your birthday suit."

She laughed and splashed at him with her free hand.

Laughing, he splashed her back, but stopped when she squealed and dropped her arm in defense, briefly baring her full breasts. "Oh my God!" She clapped her arm around her breasts again, eyes wide. "You better not have looked."

"Oh, I definitely looked." He moved closer to her, watching her face.

Her cheeks flushed pink. "Ren!"

"What? I'm not going to lie." He'd barely gotten a glimpse of her breasts, but the image was now seared into his brain nonetheless. Full breasts, pink nipples, definitely more than a handful.

Now he wanted to see all of her, stretched out on a flat surface for him to devour. Kiss by kiss. Lick by lick. Until she was crying out his name, begging for him to stop, then begging for more.

Yelping again, she jumped suddenly, dove at him and— He gathered her close, savoring the way her breasts pressed against his chest. But he moved quickly, swiveling so he could defend her against whatever had scared her.

"What is it?"

"Ah...a fish nipped me in the butt," she whispered, still hanging on to him.

And he was definitely not letting her go. He had a wet, naked Grace plastered against him, her breasts rubbing against his chest. Was this heaven? Yeah, it had to be. Pure, utter heaven. He let his hands move lower until he was cupping her perfect ass. All this skin to skin was going to short-circuit his brain, but what a way to go.

"What are you doing?" she whispered.

His gaze landed on her mouth. "Touching you."

Now she couldn't help but stare at his mouth, and when he slid one hand up her ass, over her back, just touching her everywhere he could, she went even more still. But her breathing was erratic as she looked up at him, her green eyes bright. "Can I touch you?" Another whisper.

Oh yeah. *Heaven.* "Anywhere you want," he groaned, thrilled that she wanted him back. Goddess help him, she could do whatever she wanted to him, anytime she wanted.

She tentatively slid her hands between them, moved up, her delicate fingers skating over his chest, then back down, doing exactly what he was.

"I've fantasized about touching you for so long," he murmured, cupping her cheek. Though he wanted to just take over, crush his mouth to hers, he was going to go slow.

Grace deserved it.

"Really?"

He wasn't sure why she seemed surprised, but he nodded even as he lowered his head, brushed his mouth over hers. He'd been planning to keep things gentle, but she clutched onto his shoulders.

And his primal instinct took over as she wrapped her legs around him.

Fuuuck.

His cock was rock hard between them as her body molded to his.

As he teased his tongue against hers, nipped her, learned how she liked to be kissed, she slid her hand lower until— She tentatively gripped his erection.

He froze, pulling back, but still cupping her cheek in his palm.

"Is this okay?" Her voice was low, sensual as she wrapped her fingers around him, stroked once.

Fuck. Him.

He couldn't think, or speak. Not when she had her fingers wrapped around his cock. But he growled out what he hoped sounded like yes before he crushed his mouth to hers.

He couldn't hold back now as he claimed her mouth.

And when she stroked him again he reached up, cupped a full breast, rubbed his thumb over her already hard nipple. Maybe from the cold, but he hoped it was also from desire.

Moaning, she arched into his hold so he cupped her other breast, savored the heavy feel of them in his hands. She was so much shorter than him, but had curves he loved and wanted to explore. Right here and now.

His balls were already pulling up tight because this was Grace's hand on him, stroking him, touching him. "Sweetheart, you've gotta slow down," he rasped out against her mouth. This wasn't how he'd planned this.

He wanted her to come before him.

"Why?" She looked up at him, squeezed his cock.

And he had to focus on his words, force the words out. "Because you're going to come first. More than once. You first, sweetheart." Always.

"You're sure?" she whispered, her smile mischievous as she stroked him again.

He could scent her desire as it wound around them, knew she was enjoying this, but he needed her to come. "Yes." He was still cupping one of her breasts as he slid his other palm lower.

She stroked him again. "Tell me to stop, then."

He...couldn't.

Her smile was wicked as she started stroking him harder, working him in a fast rhythm while she watched him.

And he couldn't tear his gaze from hers, couldn't have stopped her if he'd wanted to. Which he didn't. She'd just completely taken over, and even though it was foreign to him, he loved the way she was in control.

Far too soon, he started coming in her hands, growling out her name as his release punched into him. He came hard in the water, even as he wished they weren't so deep because he wanted to rub his come on her, mark her.

When he had her underneath him, he was going to take his time with her—and have his damn pants on at first. "I'm sorry," he rasped out as he held her tight to him, grabbed her ass again as she wrapped her legs around him. He couldn't seem to loosen his grip on her.

He needed his scent on her, warning anyone else away.

"For what?" She wrapped her arms around him and he pulled her close, even as he reached between their bodies.

"For not stopping you," he murmured as he cupped her mound through the water. Oh, fuck, she was slick. But he wasn't going to do this out here where anyone could stumble on them. And even though she hadn't complained, it was colder than he'd realized. Her skin was chilled and he didn't like that.

She rolled her hips against his hold and he was just about to say screw it, and bring her to climax right here but... He paused.

Her eyes were slightly dilated as she watched him, her gaze lust-addled. "What is it?" she rasped out.

"I hear some people coming this way. Sounds like teenagers or rowdy bears," he growled.

"I can't hear anything."

"Oh, they're coming." And he wasn't happy about it.

She shoved out a sigh, ran her hand down his stomach and over his half-hard cock in disappointment "Let's go."

He gripped her hip with his hand, tugged her close. "Just because we're leaving doesn't mean we're done for the night."

Lust rolled off her, potent and wild. "Let's hurry, then."

Hell yeah.

It didn't take long for them to get dressed—and Ren gave her his T-shirt to wear, deciding to go shirtless. He wanted his come and his clothing on her. Wanted her covered in him.

"I might take a hot shower when we get back," she murmured as they hurried down the dimly lit path that would take them back to town.

He was about to say he'd join her when a cluster of a dozen teens raced past them, all in their bathing suits, whooping and shouting.

Grace giggled after they'd rushed by. "I'm really glad for your super-sonic hearing right about now. Otherwise I'd still be standing bare-ass naked in a lake when they came by."

Laughing, he took her hand in his as they turned onto a more weathered part of the footpath. He was glad too. He didn't want anyone seeing Grace naked.

No one but him.

Things had just shifted between them and he wasn't going to lose her. They'd finally crossed the line from friends to more. Now he just needed to lock her down forever.

CHAPTER TEN

Before they'd made it back to their little apartment, Ren had been called away to help with something so Grace had showered by herself. Unfortunately.

Now, as she sat in the bed in her pajamas, she was trying not to obsess over what had happened between them. She'd never been so bold in her life, but with Ren she'd had the compulsion to get him off, to make him lose control.

Now she was stuck with herself and her obsessive thoughts—and sexually frustrated. For a moment, she thought about calling one of her sisters to fill them in on her and Ren, but service was spotty here. And she wasn't sure she wanted to have this conversation where she was pretty sure their neighbors in this complex might be able to hear.

She glanced at her cell, saw the little X over the bars where she should have service. Didn't matter that witches and other supernaturals had worked to keep communications up and running—some things still didn't work well.

She could hear the faint movements of some of their neighbors in the adjoining apartments, wondered if it was bears staying here or people who simply lived here. Humans, hopefully, who wouldn't be able to overhear.

The apartment was small and nicely furnished. The bedroom and living space were all connected, so it was basically a studio. It had exposed brick walls, a king-sized bed with plain gray sheets and a bundle of blankets. There was some furniture—a bookshelf and a bench at the foot of the bed. The living area had two plush chairs in front of the fireplace. And off that was a small bathroom and a kitchen. At least the ceilings were high, giving the space a bigger feel.

And she wasn't sure why she was even thinking about it.

Sighing, she got under the covers and turned off the lamplight even as she yawned. Ren hadn't known how long he'd be gone, and while she really wanted to wait up for him, to continue what they'd started, sleep was calling her name.

Grace wasn't sure how much time had passed, but when she felt the bed dip she jerked awake. And immediately calmed when she saw it was Ren sitting on the other side of the bed.

"Hey, everything okay?" she murmured.

"Yeah, just a border issue. I'll tell you more in the morning. Go back to sleep," he whispered as he shucked his shoes.

Well, that wasn't happening now.

She sat up, not bothering with the lamp because there was enough outside light from the street streaming in through the curtains. Thankfully they had solar lights all over the town, and she'd also heard that they had access to a local power plant that had survived The Fall. Which was probably why this place had fared so well.

"You showered already?" He seemed almost disappointed as he turned toward her.

"Uh...yeah."

"Then I'll have to get my scent all over you again," he murmured as he leaned across the bed, kissed her soundly.

She'd loved it when he'd rubbed himself all over her. That had definitely been hot. But the kiss was over far too quickly, and as she started to protest, he stripped his shirt off.

"I actually need to shower. I'll be quick."

Part of her wanted to say she'd join him, but she wasn't sure she was feeling that brave. Or...maybe she was.

After he ducked into the bathroom, she stripped out of her pajamas and folded them neatly on top of her suitcase in the corner. Then she slipped back under the covers and tried not to count down in her head as she waited for him.

When the water stopped running, all her muscles went taut. She wanted Ren, no doubt about that, but...she might not be ready for sex. Things had happened so fast between them and she wanted to make sure he wanted something real before she made that jump. Gah, she needed to get out of her head, as her sisters liked to tell her. But it was hard because she liked to analyze things. Sometimes to death. With Ren it was different. He made her want to be spontaneous. Maybe she had time to put her clothes back on—

Ren stepped out of the bathroom, steam rolling out behind him in little waves.

And her mouth watered. Holy hotness, the male was just plain gorgeous. Walking, talking, raw power. He'd pulled on lounge pants, but had no shirt on and his dark hair was slicked back. The backlight of the bathroom was basically illuminating all of him, every powerful inch.

"I might not be ready for sex," she blurted, pulling the covers up to her neck, feeling stupid saying this now that she'd gotten totally naked. She wasn't trying to be confusing—she was just trying to process her own emotions.

"That's okay." His voice was dark and delicious as he approached the bed, every inch the predator. "I'm not ready either."

"Really?"

He snorted as he slid onto the bed, stretched out next to her. "No, not really. If you're ready, I'm definitely ready to sink inside you. But we don't have to do anything at all. I do want to hold you, however. Come here," he murmured, motioning for her to slide closer.

"I'm naked," she whispered.

His grin was definitely wicked, sending a ribbon of warmth curling through her. "Yeah, I figured since your clothes are stacked neatly over there."

He really was observant. Feeling her cheeks heat, she scooted closer and curled up next to him, enjoying his warmth and the feel of being skin to skin with him. Just touching him turned her on, made her reconsider everything. "So what happened tonight?" she murmured against his chest, resisting the urge to slide her fingers lower.

He sighed as he trailed a hand down her bare spine. She loved how easily they'd fallen into whatever this was. They'd been friends for a while so she'd thought this might be weird.

But it was weirdly *right*.

"Food has been going missing along some border areas. It's not hurting anyone right now, but this has the potential to turn into something serious, so Logan's trying to stop it before it does."

She slid her hand up his chest, liked that she had the right to touch him. And just because she wasn't ready for sex didn't mean they couldn't be physical. "You guys will figure it out." She had no doubt. "Even though I'm not ready for sex, could we maybe do...other stuff," she whispered.

Ren moved so fast she could barely blink before he had her pinned underneath him, his dark eyes flashing with hints of amber. "I want to taste between your legs, to make you come. More than once." His words came out as a raspy growl.

She blinked, her heart rate kicking up as she nodded. That sounded...amazing. But... "Are we moving too fast?"

"Not for me." He paused, as if he wanted to say more, but then cleared his throat. He still didn't move off her, his big body pinning her in place, and she liked the weight of him on her. "But we don't have to do anything at all. Everything that happens is your call."

"No, I like...what you just said." She wanted to do that.

He smiled then, slow and wicked. "What I just said?"

"Yep."

"Say the words," he murmured, his eyes on her mouth. "Tell me exactly what you want me to do."

Ooohh. Her cheeks heated as she stared at him. She'd never been a talker in bed, and if she was being honest, she didn't have much experience. And the experience she did have had been more disappointing than anything. Her vibrator had always gotten her off a heck of a lot faster and more reliably than anyone else could.

But looking into Ren's dark eyes, she knew without a doubt that he wouldn't be disappointing.

When she didn't respond fast enough, he brushed his lips over hers, nipping her bottom lip. "That's okay," he whispered. "I'm going to get you to talk eventually. To tell me all the dirty things you want me to do to you."

Heat rushed between her legs at his words and she wrapped her arms around him as he devoured her mouth. Unfortunately the covers were in the way but thankfully he had the same thought. Without taking his mouth off hers, he shoved the blankets off and started kissing a scorching path down her neck, lower and lower.

The cool air rushed over her body, making her very aware of how naked she was. When he sucked one of her hard nipples into his mouth, she didn't think about anything but the raw pleasure of him kissing her.

As he flicked his tongue over the hard bud, he reached between their bodies and cupped her mound, teasing, stroking.

She dug her fingers into his back as he slid a finger inside her, the sensation sending a shock of pleasure through her.

She'd thought about what it would be like with Ren, but it had always been more abstract. This was...everything. And she was scared to ask what this meant to him, if he wanted more or if he wanted something casual.

When he slid another finger inside her, she sucked in a breath at the feel of him stretching her.

He murmured something against her breast that she couldn't make out before he moved lower until he was crouched between her spread legs.

She felt so vulnerable in that moment, but when he looked up at her the lust in his gaze was potent and all-consuming.

"I've been fantasizing about you like this, but the reality is so much better. You have the prettiest pussy."

She blinked at his words, but couldn't even think of a response—was there one?—before he dipped his head between her legs and flicked his tongue against her clit.

"Ren," she groaned as she rolled her hips against his face.

He began moving his fingers inside her as he teased her with his tongue, his movements slow. Too slow.

"I need you to go faster," she said, surprising herself. She normally had a problem vocalizing what she needed but Ren made her feel safe in a way no one ever had.

He started moving his fingers in a steadier rhythm, pushing deeper. "Soon it's going to be my cock inside you," he said against her in that growly voice, sending a little reverberation through her.

And her inner walls tightened at the thought, another rush of heat punching through her.

He growled again and this time he sucked on her clit, teasing her relentlessly. As he did, pleasure started building inside her.

Her climax rose up, the pleasure rolling through her as he kept going, kept teasing, until she lost it, crying out his name as he pumped his fingers inside her. Sucked on her clit. Focused on her pleasure.

Blinking as she slowly came down from the high he'd given her, she stared at him as he crawled up her body, the feel of his covered erection thick against her abdomen as he pinned her in place.

She wrapped her entire body around him then, digging her feet into his ass. "That was amazing."

"We're just getting started."

Laughing lightly, she brushed her lips over his. "I can only come once but..." She reached between them and rubbed a hand over his thick erection.

But he clasped her wrist, tugging her hand away. "That sounds like a challenge."

She grinned at the gleam in his dark eyes. "Uh, no, just reality. Besides, it's your turn."

Her stubborn jaguar just shook his head, cupped her mound again, slid two fingers inside her. Then he brought his fingers to his mouth, sucked on them. "You're coming again."

"Ren—"

He covered her mouth with his, doing that whole jaguar growl thing that made her insane. Part of her was so scared that this was going to spectacularly blow up in her face, that she was going to lose her best friend.

But the other part of her was so hopeful that this was the start of something real. Something forever.

"Will you sit on my face?" he asked against her mouth.

The blunt question sent another rush of heat spiraling through her—this time to her face. God, he just put it out there, was so bold.

And she wanted to be bold too. She nodded against his kisses, and in response he shifted with that liquid ease so that he was underneath her and she was straddling his waist.

He stretched out on his back, every inch a god as he looked up at her. "I want you right here." Her damp braid had fallen between her breasts and he tugged on it once. "Now."

Oooh, yes. She liked the way he was demanding, even as she was surprised by how much she liked it. Normally she didn't like anyone telling her what to do, but Ren was different.

Ren was everything.

Even though she felt a little self-conscious moving up his body, she quickly lost her worry as he groaned against her spread lips.

The way he flicked his tongue against her, ate at her as if he was worshipping her, was the most erotic thing she'd ever experienced. Her inner walls started tightening again, desperate to be filled by him.

As if he read her mind, he reached up from behind and curled a finger into her, thrusting slowly as he continued to tease her with his tongue.

She held on to the bed frame as he started picking up a rhythm, and cried out when he withdrew his finger.

But just as quickly, he pressed his finger against a more intimate place. She tensed, but when he said, "Is this okay?" in that sweet Ren voice, she nodded.

If he asked her just right, she'd probably say yes to anything. And that was terrifying. "Yes," she finally gasped out.

And when he pressed his finger inside her, using her own come as lubrication to push deep, everything inside her sort of...exploded in pleasure at the foreign sensation.

He sucked on her clit again and even though she should be done for the night, a climax slammed into her at the dual sensations of his finger and mouth.

All her muscles were pulled taut as she came, the pleasure rolling through her until she just collapsed on top of him.

Laughing lightly, he held her close to him, his mouth right against hers. "I knew you could come again."

She curled up against the heat of him, stroked her fingers over his chest, lower, until she dipped below his jogging pants.

Of course he wasn't wearing anything underneath. "You're going to come too." She bit his bottom lip to punctuate her point. Because while she loved that he was giving her pleasure, seemed sort of obsessed with it, she wanted to give it to him too.

Having him lose control in the lake had been amazing and she wanted to see that expression on him again, wanted to bring him as much pleasure as he'd just brought her.

Feeling almost high from her orgasms, she clasped his erection tight, began stroking him as she watched him.

His eyes flickered between jaguar and man as he stared at her, his breathing growing more and more erratic the harder she stroked.

She could see when he was close, the way his jaw tightened, the way he swallowed hard and she squeezed even harder. "Come all over me," she whispered, not sure where the words had come from.

But it set him off all the same. He growled her name as he began coming all over her, rubbing himself over her stomach and chest before he pinned her beneath him.

Then he absolutely devoured her. There was no other word for the way he kissed her. No, he was claiming her, or at least it felt like it.

And she found she very much wanted to be claimed by Ren. Forever.

CHAPTER ELEVEN

Grace zipped up her suitcase and set it back in the corner even as she tried not to obsess over where Ren was. She'd woken up alone half an hour ago and...couldn't believe that he'd just left. Not without a note or something.

She looked at her phone—still no service—and saw that she needed to leave in a few minutes. She was dressed and had everything she needed. Except Ren.

When the door jangled and the lock slid open, she paused, relief hitting her hard as Ren stepped inside, two thermoses in his hands.

"Morning, sunshine." The low timbre of his voice this morning did all sorts of things to her insides.

She'd been wondering how this morning would be after last night— oh my God, after she'd sat on his face. That had been such an amazing experience and she wanted to do it again as soon as possible. But she'd been feeling off-kilter since, wondering if things would be weird between them. "Morning yourself," she murmured, crossing the room as he came toward her.

He took away all worry as he claimed her mouth, sweet and sensually, before he pulled back with a groan. "I'd meant to be back quicker," he said, handing her one of the thermoses. "I got you hot coffee with actual flavored creamer. The kind you like."

"Creamer?" She hadn't seen that luxury anywhere in ages.

"A human family has a dairy farm and supplies the area."

"You just became my new favorite person."

"I wasn't already your favorite person?" His mouth kicked up at the corners as he took a sip of his own coffee.

"After last night you definitely are." She took a sip of her own drink, sighed in appreciation.

He snorted out a laugh. "And after last night I really hate that we're not working together today."

"What are you doing today anyway?" she asked as he held out a small cloth bag for her.

"There are a couple nutrient-dense nut bars in there for breakfast and even lunch if you need," he said. "And to answer your question, I'm heading out to the far reaches of the perimeter with Griff and a couple other shifters."

She hated the thought of him out there, unable to be contacted. She knew he was skilled and deadly, had seen it firsthand, but she was still going to worry. "Thank you, that's really thoughtful."

He just watched her for a long moment, his dark eyes hungry. For her. "I really wish we could just stay inside all day."

"Me too." She went up on tiptoe, kissed him again before pulling back. Then she tucked the bars into her backpack and slid it on her back. While she wanted to ask him what the future held for them, it felt too soon. And besides, if she didn't like the answer, she didn't want to know before heading off to work. "But we're here for a job."

Sighing, he headed toward the door. "I wish my job was making you climax all day," he murmured as he opened the door.

Aaaand they found themselves face-to-face with their neighbor across the hall. A tall male who might be a bear, but she couldn't know for sure. He was a big, bearded guy dressed in jeans and a flannel shirt. Heck, maybe he was just a big human.

The guy simply nodded at them, clearly trying to smother a smile as he locked up his own door. So yeah, he'd overheard Ren for sure.

Grace just snickered to herself and took another sip of coffee as Ren locked up their room. Then they waited until the guy disappeared down the hallway and the stairs. "I wish that was your job too," she said as soon as it was just the two of them.

He made grumbling sounds even as they headed downstairs.

She'd opted for jeans, work boots, and had layered a flannel over her tank top in case the weather decided to be moody. "Do you have any idea how long you guys will be?"

"Not really, but if you need me for anything, just ask one of the bears. I know Logan will be able to get ahold of me if our phones don't work."

"So far mine doesn't have good service."

"Yeah, mine's hit or miss," he said as they stepped outside into the cool morning air.

She was glad she'd added an extra layer now as they headed down Main Street. He took her hand in his, twining his fingers through hers, and something inside her settled at the feel of his touch, the small claiming.

"Well, I'm meeting Koa," she said as they reached the end of the street. She pointed in the opposite direction he seemed to be headed. "We're going to be working on kitting out some new greenhouses today. And I'm going to talk to an architect about possibly mimicking what we've done in New Orleans with The Grove building. A future project, but it'd be cool if they did something like that here."

Ren cupped her cheek in response, kissed her slowly before he pulled back. "Be safe today."

"I will. You too."

"Always." He looked as if he wanted to say more, but he kissed her instead, then loped off in that very feline way of his.

She forced herself not to stare and pant after him like a lovesick fool. Even if that was exactly what she was. Oh God, she did love him. Had for a long time.

The realization slammed into her. Of course she loved him.

And now...she wanted to know exactly what they were. But shifters had different norms for relationships. Dang it, she wished her phone was working because then she could call her brother-in-law. He was a dragon, a male, and could answer her questions. And he was super blunt too, so she could trust him to be honest. Or she could call any number of her shifter friends.

Shaking those thoughts away, she smiled when she reached the little complex where Koa lived, found her already waiting outside. "Hey, thanks for waiting for me."

Koa grinned, holding up a big metal thermos similar to hers. "No problem. I see you got some coffee already."

"And I'm going to enjoy every bit of it."

Koa snickered. "A woman after my own heart."

As they headed down the street, the female from the day before who'd run the food truck appeared as if out of nowhere.

"Oh, hey Estrid," Koa said, her smile brightening even wider.

"Hey." The female nodded at Grace, much the same as yesterday—curtly. Not rude or anything, but it was clear she was only interested in talking to Koa.

"What are you doing this morning?"

"Escorting the two of you around today," Estrid answered.

"Oh, that's nice... Is everything okay?" Koa's expression darkened slightly.

Grace was glad Koa had asked because she'd been wondering about those border issues Ren had mentioned.

"Oh yeah." The female smiled, a real one. "I'm just off today and Logan said I could help out."

Grace hid a grin. She was pretty sure "help out" meant spend time with Koa.

As they reached the end of the street they veered off across a field, and as the two females started chatting, Grace got all up in her head, obsessing over every single thing Ren had said to her over the last twenty-four hours.

She liked things spelled out and she knew she should have just asked him this morning if they were exclusive, but then he'd kissed her and brought her food and she just forgot to think.

"What's that look?" Koa asked, her tall friend still silent next to them.

Grace blinked, realized Koa was talking to her as they clomped through the wet grass. She was glad she'd worn her waterproof hiking boots. "What?"

"That look. It's speculative."

She felt her cheeks heat up, then cursed her Irish heritage. "Ah...just obsessing over my current 'relationship status' with a certain shifter," she admitted.

Koa laughed. "Ah, relationship status. I remember when life was so much simpler."

Which made Grace giggle. "Right? God. I haven't thought about... any of that stuff until the last few months. Now I'm just obsessing and being a weirdo. Just ignore me."

"No way. Is it one of the males from yesterday?"

"Yeah. Ren."

"Ah, I kinda thought so. His expression went all murder when you left with Logan."

Grace blinked. "Seriously?"

Koa laughed again and Estrid actually cracked a smile, nodding in agreement.

"What is your concern with the jaguar?" Estrid asked.

"Ah...where we stand, I guess. I know shifters have different rules and stuff from humans and dating. And I know I should have just asked him. I'm going to. I really am. But..." She shrugged. "I have an analytical brain and can get caught up sometimes."

"Does the male bring you food? Little gifts? Show up all the time?"

"Yes...to *all* of those things."

"He is courting you, then. He wants to feed you, take care of you. The food thing is a big deal with shifters."

"It is?" Koa blinked, looked at Estrid in surprise.

Who nodded, giving her a very interesting look.

Oooh, so Koa hadn't realized Estrid was into her? Grace cleared her throat. "Thanks. So how long are you here? I've seen you around in the city and I know you're one of Logan's people."

"I'm here as long as I'm here." Estrid lifted a shoulder, her answer completely opaque.

Okay, then.

Koa frowned so Grace moved the conversation in a different direction even as her thoughts were consumed with Ren.

CHAPTER TWELVE

"What is it?" Griff murmured, his voice subvocal so that only Ren could hear him.

"Maybe nothing." Ren eyed the thicket of bushes and trees near the territory line. There was no actual dividing line, just an area that King had decided was as far as his people's territory stretched. A stream running alongside a bunch of fields and orchards was the dividing line, and past it a few miles in the other direction were supposedly burned-down towns, destroyed forests. Ren hadn't ventured that far yet, but he trusted King's people had done the recon.

He eyed the thick oak trees twenty yards away, watched the way the green leaves rustled in the breeze. Something was off, he just couldn't figure it out.

"Ooh, shit. Something's in the trees," Griff said as quietly as before. "Middle one. With the cluster of azaleas at the bottom."

Ren couldn't see anything, but he trusted his gut. And more than that, he trusted Griff, the best tracker he knew. Right about now he wished he'd brought his magical arrows, but Logan hadn't thought there was a need. The team here just wanted to get to the bottom of the thievery with as little issue as possible.

"Just my imagination," Griff finally said, turning from the trees to look back at the stream. He'd spoken louder this time, but Ren knew he was lying. "Let's keep tracking." An orchard had been robbed last night, three of its trees massacred, as if whatever had taken and eaten the apples had been a true savage.

He and Griff headed west, farther away from the orchard they'd just left not too long ago, using the stream to guide them.

About ten minutes later, Ren silently started stripping and Griff did the same. They moved quickly, changing into their animal form. Since they'd been working together for over a century—both when they'd been recruited for black ops and when they'd grown up in the same pack together—they already had a plan of attack.

And this one was simple. Shift, double back, and find out what the heck was up in those trees. Ren took to the nearest tree while Griff's wolf blended with the shadows in a way that still awed Ren.

His friend seemed to meld into the forest, becoming part of it in a way that defied logic. Ren was nimble on his feet and stuck to the high branches, moving fast as he headed back the way they'd come.

There were other teams out tracking right now but they each had a designated zone they were supposed to stick to as they searched out possible tracks. But so far there hadn't been any tracks. Just weird dragging marks that Griff thought might be wings. Unfortunately they were too small to be dragon, so it ruled that out. And there'd been no traces of fire or anything left behind, so—

Ren paused on the tree next to the one he'd been staring at before.

He crept along the branch, his paws quiet as he looked for the perfect jumping point. Because something was in that oak tree, lurking in the shadows. As he prepared to run and jump, a flurry of...*something* attacked him.

He could hear wings flapping as something squawked and squeaked, knocking him off the branch with a giant swipe.

Shit.

He twisted in midair, landed on a weak branch, used it as a springboard. As it started to crack, he dove for a bigger one.

As he landed on it, the wings hit him again in the face. The invisible fucking wings, knocking him down the six feet to the ground.

KATIE REUS

He landed on all fours, let out a snarl.

Griff raced at him from the shadows, jumped into the air and bit something Ren couldn't see.

Another yelp rent the air, then there was an explosion of colors, nearly blinding Ren before the colors disappeared amid the sound of rapid-fire flapping.

Ren jumped in the air, trying to grab whatever the heck Griff had just bit, but no luck.

"It's gone," Griff said as he crouched, deeply inhaling as he stood.

Ren shifted too. "What the hell was that?"

"I don't know. It—and this is weird to say—tasted like a dragon. So maybe it is a dragon we're dealing with."

"A small dragon—fuck, a dragonling, maybe?" Oh hell, that changed everything.

"I think so. But I don't know what was up with that rainbow flash." Griff made a sort of spitting motion, wiped his mouth. "Goddess, I feel bad if that was a dragonling."

Yeah, because they didn't hurt younglings, cubs, pups, kids. It was ingrained in them. You simply didn't do that. They were to be protected, always.

"You're bleeding,"

"What?" Ren looked down, saw his arms had been shredded. And now that he was coming off his burst of adrenaline, he realized that his back hurt too. He turned around. "How bad is it?"

"Yikes on bikes."

Ren let out a startled laugh, winced at the lance of pain as he turned back around. "What did you just say?"

Griff just shrugged. "I dunno, I heard one of the wolf pups say it the other night."

"Dude, don't say that again. It sounds ridiculous."

"Yikes on bikes, your fucking back is sliced up. Also, yikes on bikes," Griff added. Because sometimes he was a wolfy asshole.

Ren rolled his eyes at him. "You're ridiculous."

"And you need to get cleaned up."

"I can help with that," a female voice called out. One of the healers on

72

patrol with them strode out of the woods, along with a handful of other shifters. Wolves, a bear and a dragon. All in human form, but he vaguely knew them on sight, had seen them in New Orleans.

"I'm fine," he said.

"I'll be the judge of that," the petite female with dark braids said as she approached, her mouth pulled into a thin line.

He sighed because he had to listen to her; she was a healer. He gave her his back, actually wishing he had some pants.

As if Griff read his mind, he nodded at him. "I'm gonna go grab our stuff. I'll be back."

"This isn't too bad," the healer said. "You'll be healed in a couple hours. And your scars'll be gone by tomorrow. So what happened exactly?"

"We're not sure." He quickly recapped what had happened, ignoring the way a couple of the other females who'd arrived eyed him. Damn, he really wanted his pants now. He only wanted Grace's eyes on him. No one else's.

"Well, these do look like dragon claws. Small ones," she said as she cleaned around the wound in his back. "And if I had to guess, I don't think intentional. These weren't made with the intention to kill or maim. They're wilder and erratic."

"They still hurt," he grumbled, wishing he had Grace with him. She'd make him feel better. Then he felt bad for the thought because no way in hell he wanted Grace near any of this. Whatever *this* was. "And I need to report what we've seen back to Logan."

They continued talking as she cleaned up his blood, only pausing when Griff returned in wolf form, carrying Ren's clothes in his mouth. After he shifted, he said, "How are you feeling? Because I think I might be able to catch the scent."

"I'm fine."

The healer clucked behind him, but he ignored her.

"You want to go now?" Ren asked, energy buzzing through him.

Griff nodded then shifted back to wolf.

"Can you relay everything to Logan, tell him we're going to try to hunt down the dragonling, see if we can find what's going on?" Ren said to the healer.

She nodded. "Yes, but be careful. I know you'll heal but try not to make it worse."

"I'll be careful," he said, wishing he could remember her name. "And we'll carry our packs. Let Logan know we'll reach out if we need."

"We're following you guys," one of the female wolves called out from the cluster of shifters already stripping and shifting.

Ren ignored her. He didn't know those shifters well, and he and Griff were fine on their own. But if they wanted to follow, whatever. They'd have to keep up.

He shifted to his jaguar, the magic of the change invigorating him, helping speed up the healing process immediately. Then he raced off into the woods, trailing Griff and the mysterious dragonling.

The sooner they figured out this mystery, the sooner he could get back to Grace. His female.

CHAPTER THIRTEEN

Grace's heart skipped a beat, as it always did when she saw Ren. She hadn't seen him since this morning—and an entire day was far too long not to get her Ren fix. It was like her body was just attuned to him as he jogged up to the bench where she was eating with Koa and Estrid, his hair damp, an easy smile on his face. She had to actively fight not to melt into a puddle.

"Hey," she murmured as he reached her. "When did you shower?" Because she'd just been back at their place and had sadly showered alone.

He gave her one of those wicked smiles and had started to respond when a tall, dark-haired female strode up and handed him a small bag. "Hey, you left this in the shower." Her voice was all inviting and she very intentionally trailed her fingers down Ren's forearm.

Grace froze, ice coating her veins. *Wait...what?*

"Ren!"

They both turned at Logan's shout. He was hurrying toward them, his expression intense.

Grace felt weird, almost numb as she tried to process what that female had said. The shower? Had Ren been in there with her? It made Grace feel ill.

"Shit, I gotta go," Ren murmured, his expression apologetic. "I won't be long."

Grace was suddenly aware of the two females watching her across the table as sounds and the setting seemed to rush back into her consciousness.

She pushed back and stood. "You guys can have my food if you want. I'm good."

Koa frowned, her gaze flitting in the direction Ren had gone, then back to Grace. "The bears are having a get-together tonight. You should come. We're heading that way in about fifteen minutes. Nothing crazy, just a bonfire and s'mores and stuff. Come on, I don't want to be the only human there."

"Yes, join us," Estrid said, taking a sip of her beer, her expression sincere. The bear shifter had warmed up to Grace today, probably because it was clear she wasn't vying for Koa's attention. "There will be many handsome bears there. And bears are better than all other shifters." Her mouth curved up ever so slightly.

Grace snorted, but it made her smile. "Fine, I'll go."

"You sound like we've invited you to be tortured," Koa said.

Grace snickered, even as pain lanced through her chest. Ren wouldn't have showered with someone else. Right? Maybe... She was trying to think what the woman could have meant and not jump to conclusions. But that female had very intentionally touched Ren, Grace wasn't imagining that. She'd touched him like she had a right to.

And Grace was glad she didn't have claws because she quite literally wanted to claw the female's face off. The violent reaction shocked her, but maybe she'd been hanging out with shifters too long.

Or maybe shifters had the right idea. If someone messed with her man, clawing them up sounded really good.

"I'm going to need alcohol tonight," she murmured.

Estrid grinned and popped open the cooler she'd been carrying around. "I've got you covered."

∾

"WHAT THE HECK did you give me?" Grace plopped down in the Adirondack-style chair next to Estrid, who was nursing a beer and watching Koa across the bonfire talking to someone they worked with. Her expression was one of quiet yearning.

"Cider. The recipe has been in my family for generations."

"Is the alcohol content high?" Because she was feeling a buzz after two drinks. To be fair, she hadn't had much alcohol in years and was a lightweight on a good day.

Estrid looked at her, tilted her head slightly to the side. "For you, probably yes." Then she plucked the drink from her hand.

"Hey!"

"You're small and I didn't take that into consideration."

"I'm not that small," she grumbled as she took the water Estrid pulled from her magical cooler.

Estrid just gave her a dry look and went back to watching Koa.

"So…why haven't you made a move on Koa yet?" There were a ton of people at the bonfire, though she hadn't seen Ren yet. Or that female who'd touched him like she had a right to.

Estrid gave her a surprised look. "Alcohol makes you nosy."

"True. I also have sisters and we talk about everything. And I've decided that you're my friend now. So no stoic bear routine for you tonight. What's up with you two?" Because all day they'd been giving each other covert looks when the other wasn't looking. It was adorable.

Estrid sighed, took a sip of her cider. "She's just recently been introduced to the world of supernaturals. She knew of us of course, because of The Fall. But…I don't want to scare her off or make her feel pressured. I like being her friend."

As if she knew they were talking about her, Koa looked over, the flames of the bonfire licking up between them. She smiled sweetly at both of them before the male she was talking to drew her attention back.

"Friend, schmend." Grace stood, had to take stock of herself for a moment when she weaved once, realized she was okay. Then she grabbed her water and made her way around the bonfire to Koa and

Robert, the talker. He'd worked with them today, and while he was so nice, he just didn't have an off switch.

"I'm sorry to interrupt, but Koa, Estrid needs to talk to you," she said as she came up to them.

Koa looked relieved at the interruption, and hurried off with an apology, but that meant Grace got to talk to Robert. Which was how she ended up being a captive audience to a male who was telling her all about the bird boxes he'd been building for owls. And okay, it was pretty interesting because she liked owls, and obscure nerdy facts in general, but she still wondered where Ren was.

Off with that female?

Grace frowned at herself, but then blinked when she saw Koa sitting in Estrid's lap, their faces close to each other, the bear shifter actually smiling. *Nice.*

At least someone was happy tonight.

"I have another gift for you," Logan said, appearing out of the crowd, slinging his big arm around her shoulders.

She blinked up at him. "What?" The noise level was slowly, steadily rising as more shifters arrived to the outdoor party.

"Well, not for you, but for my princess."

She snickered at his nickname for the human. "Ah. Whatever you have for her, just add it to the pile and I'll make sure she gets it. But I think I'm going to have to charge you a fee for—"

"Nope." Ren was suddenly there, pushing Logan's arm off Grace's shoulder. "No touching."

Grace's mouth fell open as he placed himself between her and Logan.

"Touch my female again and I'm going to fuck up that handsome face," Ren snarled.

"Ren!" Grace gasped.

Logan threw his head back and laughed. "I am sorry, my friend," he finally said, clapping Ren on the shoulder. "I'm an affectionate bear."

"Keep your affection to yourself."

"Of course. I apologize." Logan held up his palms in surrender, winked at Grace then disappeared back into the crowd of partygoers.

"What the hell was that?" Grace demanded, rounding on Ren. "You can shower with someone but a friend harmlessly puts his arm around me and you're threatening to hurt him?"

"Shower with someone?" Ren stared at her as if she'd lost her mind.

"That female brought you stuff you 'left in the shower,'" she said in a slightly mocking tone because that cider had really gone to her head. And okay, she was just pissed. He'd disappeared over an hour ago. "And don't tell me I'm crazy. I heard what she said and then she touched you in an intimate way." Right in front of Grace.

His expression was still one of shock. "I took a shower in the communal warrior's gym—but they have individual stalls with curtains. I didn't shower with anyone! And I already told that female not to touch me again."

"Oh." She blinked. "You did?"

"Yes." He reached out, gently gripped her hips. "I don't want anyone but you. I thought that was clear by now."

She sucked in a breath at his words, hearing the truth. "I don't want anyone but you either," she murmured, sliding her arms around him as he pulled her close.

"You got kinda jealous," he murmured, his gaze on her mouth.

"Yeah...it's a new sensation." And she didn't like it.

"It's kind of hot." His wicked grin was back.

"How about you don't give me a reason to be jealous in the future?"

His expression went serious. "Never."

She swallowed hard, and decided to just ask about the female she'd seen at his house before they'd left on this trip. The party was in full swing and it was clear that no one was paying attention to them, not when a group of bears was having a dance-off about thirty yards away. And even if someone overheard, she didn't really care. "So...you said you weren't dating anyone before we left New Orleans and I believe you. But...I came to your house on Friday morning and saw you hugging a female outside your house. It seemed pretty serious." And dating and fucking were two different things.

"Friday?" He blinked, frowned, then let out a short laugh. "Oh, that was Destiny. She was one of the females we rescued from...that place. She stopped by to update me on how she's been doing, that's all. She doesn't trust many supernaturals, even now, but she's doing well. And all we did was hug, which you must have seen."

Oooh. Grace knew about that, hated that humans had been trafficked, and through King's territory, no less. "God, I feel so stupid now," she murmured, burying her face against his chest. "I thought she must have stayed the night or something. It was so early and then you guys were hugging and…" She groaned as she pulled back and looked up at him.

"I'm glad to know you cared enough to get annoyed. Wait, is that why you said you were on a date?"

"I didn't text that, Luna did. She said you deserved to think I was dating."

Ren snort-laughed, leaned down to brush his mouth over hers. "So we're good? Because I don't like seeing you jealous or worried. I never want to make you feel like I could be with anyone else."

"So we're exclusive, then?" Because she really, really needed it spelled out. Maybe in skywriting. Or by fire dancers.

His grip on her hips tightened. "I don't share, Grace. And I will never, ever share you. I've wanted you from the moment I saw you. I only held off courting you because I thought you'd sworn off males."

A shiver rolled down her spine, heat punching through her at the possessiveness in his tone. "I wish I could go back in time and tell my former self to shut up about that. And for the record, I won't share you either. And don't you forget it."

"Never." His eyes were molten as he stared at her, his intentions clear. "Do you want to get out of here?

"Oh yeah." Nothing compared to alone time with Ren.

CHAPTER FOURTEEN

R en held Grace close as the shower poured down around them, not wanting to let her go. But they both had to get to work.

"Ugh, I just want to stay inside with you all day," Grace grumbled, mirroring his thoughts.

Last night after they'd cleared up that Ren wasn't seeing anyone and didn't want to see anyone but Grace, they'd fooled around more back in the privacy of the apartment. And it was so damn nice that they had this space for just the two of them. She wasn't ready for sex yet, but that was fine with him.

She was his, regardless. And vice versa.

"Let's just call in sick."

She pinched his ass, then leaned forward to turn the shower off. "I wish. We'd be the biggest jerks though if we did."

He slid his hands down her back and over her butt, then back up again, reveling in the sensation of touching her everywhere he wanted. They might not be mated, but he'd put his scent on her multiple times. Everyone here would scent that she was off-limits. "I'm trying to care," he murmured as he tugged back the shower curtain and grabbed two towels for her. One for her hair, the other for her body.

She giggled as she wrapped her hair up first. "They'd know we were lying, which would be even worse."

As she wrapped the second towel around herself, he snagged one for himself and began drying off, even as she started doing all the little routine bathroom things—lotioning her arms and legs, then putting a different kind on her face. She had a whole routine and it sort of fascinated him.

His was a lot simpler, but he loved watching her get ready. Still, he needed to get her coffee and feed her and now was the only time to do it. "I'm going to grab us coffee and food while you get ready."

"You're the best."

"True," he murmured, kissing her soundly. "And I take payments for my awesomeness in sexual favors."

She laughed loudly, the sound music to his ears as he hurried from the bathroom.

After drying off, he tossed his clothes on and hurried down to the closest local center that had coffee and nutrient-dense bars. They were okay as far as flavor went, but there were a lot of calories, good for the full days they were putting in.

By the time he got back upstairs, Grace was sadly dressed, her damp hair pulled into a braid and her backpack at the foot of the bed. "I finally got ahold of my sisters," she said as she took the coffee he gave her.

And he kissed her again because he couldn't help himself. "Everything good at home?"

"Yes, and they're happy about us." She grinned at him and he felt that look and the scent rolling off her all the way to his core.

He'd never thought it was possible to feel so much, to be so happy, but he knew on a molecular level that Grace was his mate. Had known from the beginning.

But now that she reciprocated... It was a lot to process. He wanted to tell her that he loved her, but he knew it was too soon. Shifters and humans were different that way. "Not as happy as me," he said, tucking the bars he'd gotten into the side of her backpack. He wanted to make sure she had enough food. And since he couldn't be with her today, he'd take care of her in small ways.

She slipped her hand in his. "Or me. But they're still happy, especially Nana. She very smugly said 'Glad he finally made a move,' so apparently my grandmother is more astute than me."

"Than all of us," he said as he opened the door, snagging his arrow sheath and bow as they left.

"You're bringing your arrows today?" A hint of worry bled into Grace's voice.

"Yeah, but just because I feel naked without them."

"I like you naked," she murmured.

He let out a startled laugh. "The feeling is mutual."

Though he hated to do it, downstairs he parted ways with Grace since Koa was waiting, but it was hard.

So. Fucking. Hard.

He could just fake sickness, say he needed a day in bed. And Grace was the only one who could nurse him back to health. *You're a dumbass,* his jaguar growled. *But I still like the plan.*

He was so caught up in his thoughts as he made his way to the meeting point, he was surprised to find only Logan and not Griff or the others. Ren tensed. "Is this about threatening your face? Because I don't feel like fighting this morning. I'm in too good a mood."

Logan just laughed. "My face is threatened all the time by the wolves. I'm used to it. I get that males simply cannot handle this level of handsomeness. It is not your fault."

Ren narrowed his eyes ever so slightly. Last night Grace had told him Logan was sending back some letters and gifts to a human female named Zia through Grace. Ren was relatively new to the territory and hadn't realized the bear was into someone. "Yes, that must be it. Or maybe it's the fact that you were touching my female. Next time I'm in New Orleans I'll return the favor and give Zia a big hug." Lies—he didn't even know the female. And he wouldn't be hugging any female but Grace. And probably Grace's nana, but that was it.

For the first time, Logan's eyes went pure bear. Just as quickly, the man was back as he glared at Ren. "Fine. I see your point. But I am affectionate. It's a bear thing and I meant no disrespect. If I thought my embrace had been unwelcome, I would never have hugged her. Or anyone for that matter. I respect boundaries."

"I know." And it was fucking annoying how nice the bear was. "I was just off-balance last night because we hadn't figured things out between us yet."

"That, I do understand."

Ren nodded once. "So what's up? Are we waiting on anyone?" He glanced around the area, could scent bears and wolves and a few humans nearby, but this close to the entrance of the hiking reserve he couldn't see anyone.

"Nope. You're working with me today. A wolf expressed an interest in Griff so I paired them up."

"I didn't take you for a matchmaker," Ren said as they started down the path.

"I love love. What can I say? According to my mama, my heart is big and romantic."

Ren just smiled. Freaking male bears. More in touch with their emotions than any other shifters on the planet.

GRACE CROUCHED DOWN NEXT to Koa, picked up the burned, charred pear lying on the ground. "This isn't good," she murmured.

"No. Way too close to our greenhouses." Koa glanced behind them and Grace did the same.

They couldn't actually see the greenhouses or the other orchards and fields this close to the forest line, but...whatever was happening here looked a lot like what Ren had told her about last night. "We need to contact Logan." He was in charge of the whole territory for now. King had sent him here because of his personality and the fact that he was a natural-born Alpha. If he wanted, he could run this area permanently and Grace had a feeling King would be fine with it.

Koa pulled out her walkie-talkie and spoke into it quickly, telling Logan exactly where they were.

As she spoke, Grace stared as a little dragonling came into focus at the tree line. *Holy. Shit.*

She lived with a dragon so she was more or less used to them, but... this little one had been blending into the trees with an impressive camouflage. It was the size of a small horse, but it seemed too skinny. It had a silvery coloring, but kept sort of...flashing, with other colors. As if it couldn't hold on to one color for long.

She took a step forward, palms out, and the dragonling disappeared from view. But she knew it was there, now that she was looking right in its direction. "Do you need help?" she asked quietly as she took another couple steps toward it.

"Uh, Grace?"

"Slow movements only," she murmured to Koa, who'd come up next to her.

"Where did it go?"

"It's still there, just using a natural camo."

"Well Logan's on the way so...maybe we should just sit tight."

"We will," she said even as she sat on the grass and slid off her back-pack. She pulled out one of the nutrient bars Ren had gotten for her. "I've got some treats for you," she said in the direction of the dragonling.

It "appeared" again, this time a few feet closer. It hopped toward them once, twice. Then back again. It had a silvery gray coloring, almost shimmering under the sunlight, and clear green, intelligent eyes.

Koa sat next to her, her legs crossed as she pulled out some snacks from her pack.

Grace took a bite of her bar, then held it out to the dragonling. It was about twenty feet away now, head cocked as it watched her warily. And its wings were pulled back as if it was trying to make itself smaller. It seemed so scared.

When the little creature didn't move, she broke off a piece, then tossed it gently in the animal's direction.

It backed up. Then moved toward them again, sniffed the little treat before gobbling it up. Then it hunched down and basically army crawled toward them—as if it wasn't a fire-breathing predator.

"This is the cutest thing ever but I'm also kinda scared," Koa murmured in a soothing tone.

"Yeah, me too." A scared animal could be unpredictable, but it was clear this little baby was terrified. And too skinny. It was probably starving, trying to live on its own in the woods and simply too scared to come near people or shifters. There were a couple dragonlings living in New Orleans and she knew that their mentalities were like that of small children.

When it was about five feet from them, she held out the rest of her bar.

The dragonling stopped, watched her with those clear green eyes.

"You've gotta come closer if you want it."

Instead, it scooted back.

"Oh, I see how it is. I guess I'll just eat it by myself." She lifted it to her mouth, started to take a bite, but froze when it made a whining sound.

Okay, she wasn't a monster, and if it didn't want to come any closer, she'd toss it this time. She gently threw it to the dragonling, which pounced, devoured it.

Then it kept crawling toward her, leaving drag marks behind it in the grass and dirt until finally it was right in front of them.

Grace held out her palm. "Can I pet you?" she whispered, moving her hand slowly toward it.

The dragonling flinched and she froze. Oh no, it was like it expected to be hit. She frowned even as she slowly lowered her hand toward its head, began rubbing gently behind its ear like she'd done with her friend's pet dragonling.

The little creature flopped out completely, its legs going out in all directions as it made happy little sounds.

Koa petted behind the other ear as she said, "This is the single coolest thing I've ever done."

"Don't let Estrid overhear you say that," Grace said slyly. "Because I saw you making out last night."

Koa snorted. "I can't believe you just said that."

"And I can't believe we've been working together all morning and you haven't said a word about last night. Talk, now."

"A lady never kisses and tells." Koa paused. "And since I'm not a lady, I can tell you that we are now an item. I'm still sort of stunned, but man, I've been crushing on her since she got here. She's so fucking hot and serious and I love it."

"Grace!" Ren's panicked voice sounded behind her.

The dragonling chirped, panicked, and flapped wildly, almost shoving them back as it tried to run away.

Grace glanced over her shoulder as Ren and Logan raced toward them. "You guys have to chill," she whispered because their shifter hearing would pick up everything.

"I'll circle around. I can get him from behind." This from Logan.

"No," she said as she looked back at the line of trees. That sort of shimmery outline was there.

The dragonling was still there, watching them.

"Yeah, guys. Just sit down and relax," Koa added. "You can't go all alpha right now. He's not dangerous."

"He can breathe fire." This from Ren.

"And I'm not going to hurt him," Logan added.

"But you'll still scare him and betray his trust," Grace said.

They were silent for a long moment, then she heard them sit behind her and Koa.

"We're not going to hurt you. And neither are they," she said, gesturing behind herself.

A moment later, the camouflage fell and the dragonling stared at all of them, his wings pulled up tight. It hopped toward them a few times.

Then jumped right back.

And on and on for half an hour—during which Logan fell asleep, or was at least pretending to.

Finally, the little guy crept close to her and Koa again, his body scrunched down close to the ground as he moved in for pets.

"You're just a sweet baby," Grace murmured as she pulled out another bar. As he ate it out of her hand, she scratched behind his ear.

"And I think the mystery of your big, bad attacker and the food thief has been solved."

"Hey, he's got claws," Ren grumbled even as he slowly moved in with that feline sneakiness—and petted the dragonling.

Now the little guy was full-on purring, only tensing slightly when Logan shifted to sit up.

"You've caused us quite a lot of trouble," Logan said to the dragonling.

The little creature stared at Logan, then averted his gaze, likely because Logan was an Alpha.

"I think we should see if he'll come with us." Grace slowly started getting to her feet, and as the others did the same, the dragonling moved back, but just a little.

Not like before, however. He watched them warily so Grace pointed in the direction they'd come. "We can get you set up nicely." She had no clue how much the little guy actually understood, but tone and hand motions would help a lot. She knew that much from the dragonlings back in New Orleans. "And a lot more food than just snack bars."

The dragonling hopped up and down, agitated, and shook his head, his wings flapping. He turned away from them, flapped his wings a few times.

"Am I crazy, or does he want us to follow?" Koa murmured.

When he did it again, Logan sighed. "Pretty sure you're right. He's probably got siblings. From what I understand, dragons are hatched in a group of eggs."

Grace blinked in surprise, glanced at Ren who nodded even as he pulled her close, slid his hand in hers seamlessly.

She linked her fingers through his, glad he was here. "We should follow, then."

Logan cleared his throat. "Why don't you ladies—"

"If you tell us to stay, like we're fragile females who didn't convince this little guy to get closer, you won't like the results," Koa said, a mischievous grin on her face as she eyed Logan.

Logan sighed, as if put upon. "Fine. You two follow behind us. And for the record, it's not because you're female. Or fragile," he added. "It's just that humans can be more susceptible to attack by dragon fire and I'm not certain of how well this dragonling can control himself."

"Yeah," Koa said dryly, "he's a real man-eating beast."

Grace smothered a smile since the dragonling was hopping up and down by a tree, still motioning for them to follow.

"I want to tell you to stay too," Ren said, sticking close to her. "But cats are smarter than bears."

She nudged him in the side as they all moved deeper into a triple-canopy forest that hadn't been cleared in far too long.

After they breached the other side of the forest, what had once been a neighborhood but was now just ash and rubble, the victim of a dragon attack, stretched out for what seemed like miles. Seeing the destruction was a punch to her solar plexus. Dragons had killed her parents, destroyed half the world. She certainly didn't hate all dragons—her wonderful brother-in-law was one and so were many of her friends. But being here, seeing all this, was a stark reminder of how lucky she was to have ended up in a good territory.

The dragonling stopped dead and made sad little chirping sounds, pointing west then looking up at Logan beseechingly.

"Fuck," Logan murmured, then glanced at Ren. "We haven't explored past this area. It's not part of what King wanted to claim. At least not now. There's too much destruction."

Ren gritted his teeth but didn't respond.

The dragonling chirped again, pointed in the same direction, over and over.

"We'll stay with the baby if you guys want to go check it out," Grace finally said when Ren and Logan seemed to be having a nonverbal conversation. They'd been walking for over an hour, and while she wasn't tired, she knew her limits as a human. And venturing into post-apocalyptic areas... No thanks. Not to mention, she understood that Logan and Ren could move a heck of a lot faster than they could on their own.

"Yeah, something's clearly wrong." Koa knelt down next to the drag-onling and comforted him.

Nodding, Logan pulled out his radio and tried to make a call, but got static. Koa did the same, got the same results.

"We'll run and get backup," Grace said.

Ren nodded, looking relieved. "Take the dragonling with you and find Griff."

She pulled Ren close even as she nodded. "Be safe. I mean it. No jaguar heroics or shenanigans. You come back to me," she ordered, fear taking root in her core. They'd just started this thing between them. And it was so new, she was flat-out terrified that the universe would take him away from her.

The world was so cruel sometimes and…she didn't want to lose Ren. She'd lost her parents and so many friends. She simply…couldn't deal with losing the male she was in love with.

"I'll come back to you," he growled, brushing his lips over hers briefly before he hurried off with Logan.

As they raced down the side of the hill toward the burned-out neighborhood, it hit her again how damn lucky she'd been to be in New Orleans, that they hadn't been hit like so much of the world. It looked like the remnants of a dragon apocalypse before them. And the male she loved was running right into whatever dangers lay beyond it.

CHAPTER FIFTEEN

"I didn't realize how bad it was outside our territory," Logan murmured as they stalked through what had once been a forest but was now ash, with little hints of green peeking up randomly from the blackened earth. "I've seen some videos and images, but…" He shook his head, sighed. "It's different seeing it in person, I guess."

"Some places are worse." Ren had seen an entire metropolitan city completely destroyed from dragon fire. Sometimes when he closed his eyes at night, he still saw the carnage and destruction. There had been no bodies either, just ash. The images would haunt him until the day he died.

That nothingness was… There was no word for it. It was difficult to process that many lives lost so quickly.

"I can imagine, but I don't want to see it," Logan said, shaking his head as they reached an old baseball field that had fared well enough. Part of the scoreboard was burned away as well as part of the fence, but everything else was mostly intact, if covered in pollen and dust. "You smell that?" Logan paused, stood still as they reached where a baseball diamond had once been.

Ren did the same, inhaled. Until this moment, the ash had been the only thing he'd scented, overpowering even the traces of Grace on him. "Yeah. I hear...something too." Like crying maybe. A wounded animal.

"Come on." Logan started jogging even as he glanced around their surroundings.

Ren did the same, looking for a threat as they headed for what had once been an elementary school. It was an older one-story building, with a roof caved in on one side, but the rest of the structure was solid enough.

The crying was coming from inside it or at least close by.

As they reached the edge of the building, both he and Logan peered through a dingy window. Overturned desks and faded pictures on walls greeted them, but no signs of life.

A sort of whimpering sound came from nearby.

Logan motioned that they should head along the outer wall so Ren followed, breathing in various scents. There were a handful of supernaturals nearby.

And there was no way to tell if they were friend or foe yet.

Logan suddenly stopped about ten yards from the edge of the wall. He motioned for Ren to climb and tell him what he saw.

Staying in human form, Ren jumped straight up, thankful for his jaguar strength and speed as he latched onto the edge of the flat roof and then shimmied over the edge, his movements stealthy.

He eased across the roof, the scents stronger.

"We should just move on," a male voice said, then burped, long and loud.

Ren froze, but then kept inching his way to the other side of the roof. Finally he had enough visibility to see that there was a courtyard of sorts. The elementary school's architecture had been a big square, with a courtyard in the middle of everything—a place to eat and a playground visible for all classrooms. It was a good setup and now it looked as if a group of supernaturals was using it as a place to crash.

He wasn't sure what kind they were, but they were large and their scents weren't fully human. He didn't see any humans or anyone in distress, but there was definitely a cry coming from somewhere close by.

"Not yet," a male with dark hair and a leather vest said as he tossed a bone into an unlit firepit. Trash and other debris filled it. "I want to see if we can catch that dragonling before we move on."

"Why? We've got two still and that's enough to feed us for a while." A blond male spoke now, the same voice as before.

"That little asshole isn't getting away."

There were two more males, both sitting in lawn chairs in front of the unlit firepit, and they both nodded their agreement.

Okay, so the one in the vest with the dirty beard was in charge. And they were holding dragonlings captive. Not many supernaturals would hurt kids, much less eat them, so these fuckers were going to die one way or another. Ren wanted to be the one to take the leader out. He was tempted to notch one of his arrows right now, but he'd never been one to make rash decisions.

Ren needed to talk to Logan, figure out if they wanted to take these guys on alone or wait for backup. Ren was secure in his ability to fight— he'd been in supernatural black ops for a long time—but there were a lot of unknowns right now. There could be more than four of these guys. And while his arrows were magical, would incapacitate supernaturals even as they killed them, they didn't work on everything.

Slowly, he made his way back to Logan, held up four fingers to indicate four potential threats. Then he leaned in and quietly told him everything he'd seen.

Logan paused, clearly weighing what they should do. Though Ren was alpha in nature, he wasn't an Alpha, wasn't in charge, so when it came down to it he would respect Logan's decision. Unless of course it somehow put Grace or anyone he cared about in danger. Then all bets were off.

Finally Logan leaned in, said, "You can run faster than me. Race to base, gather up a handful of shifters and bring them back here. We need a dragon too, for an aerial attack, if possible. I'll stay and keep an eye on things. If they try to hurt a dragonling, I'm going to attack no matter what. But I'll wait otherwise."

Ren didn't like the idea of leaving Logan by himself, even if the male was deadly and capable, an Alpha to his bones. But the male was right,

Ren was faster than most shifters. He nodded, then froze at the sound of male laughter coming in the direction they'd just come from.

He glanced in the direction of the baseball field, didn't see anyone, but knew they wouldn't have much time before whoever had laughed was visible.

Logan eased up one of the windows and they both dove inside the classroom. As he jumped back up, he hurried to one of the other dirty windows and peered through, waiting to see who appeared. Four males, two wearing similar vests to the other he'd seen, were stalking across the baseball field and they were carrying something.

Goddess.

He froze when he realized one of them was dragging the little dragonling behind him, his wings tangled in a net of sorts.

His thoughts immediately went to Grace—she and Koa had been with the dragonling. That was when he saw that a male straggling behind had two limp bodies over his shoulders.

No. No, no, no.

He looked over at Logan, whose eyes were pure bear now.

Ren wanted to dive out the window and run straight for them, attack. But that was beyond fucking stupid. Even as rage and fear battled inside him for dominance, he shoved everything down, locked it up.

Focus, focus. He had to focus for his female, to save her.

"There're only two ways they'll get to the courtyard," Logan said subvocally. "I'm guessing that way." He pointed in the direction the males were headed.

Ren stared out the window, wishing he had fire-breathing capabilities so he could incinerate every one of those males. On instinct he pulled out his weapon, notched one of the glowing arrows. "That piece of trash carrying Grace and Koa is in the back," he murmured, looking over at Logan. He had a feeling he knew what Logan planned, but they needed to be on the same page. "Once they pass through the opening between the two buildings, I'll be able to attack him. I'm aiming to kill immediately." The male had his hands full so it would be easier to strike him right in the chest even though Ren still risked the females getting hurt.

"Yes. They all die today. I've heard your aim is precise?"

Ren nodded, though fear still lanced through him that he would make a mistake, hurt the female he loved more than life itself. "It is."

"Okay. As soon as he's close enough, you shoot him. I'll have your back with the other males." He motioned to the doorway. "There are glass doors at the end of each hallway. I'll attack as soon as I see the male is down. Try to get the females to some sort of safety as we kill everyone."

Ren nodded, his jaw tight as he looked out the window again. There was a small timeframe he'd have, when the males moved between the buildings, to shoot the male holding Grace and Koa.

It was a pretty shitty plan, but it was all they had before they lost the element of surprise. "Go. I've got this."

As Logan moved silently into the hallway, Ren moved to the window and quietly pushed one of the desks near the open pane.

Then he half lay across it, using it for balance as he eyed the males still stalking through the grass. They were across the baseball field, still talking and laughing, their words vile and disgusting.

Ren forced himself to tune out what they were saying, how they were planning to hurt two innocent human females, as he aimed straight for the male's heart. It was a difficult angle by any standard, especially since the male had two people on his shoulders.

But the guy was broad-shouldered and wide-chested, giving Ren a good target. And he would not miss. His mate's life was in danger, and the male who had taken her would die.

He breathed out slowly, as he'd practiced a thousand times before. He'd killed hundreds with his arrows, maybe more, but never had a shot count as much as this.

Closer, closer, the males drew to the school and Ren realized he'd have to shoot before they all got into the courtyard between the buildings. If he didn't, he'd lose the only angle he had to kill the male.

He just hoped Logan was ready as...three, two, one— He let the arrow fly, was already diving through the open window before it had hit his target directly in the chest.

Everything happened so quickly as the male flew back, the arrow protruding from his chest as Grace and Koa fell to the ground without a sound.

Goddess, he refused to entertain the idea that they were anything but alive as he notched another arrow, pulled back and fired again as one of the males turned toward him, raging as he started to shift.

Slam! The arrow hit the male right between the eyes.

The male fell backward as a roar rent the air, then another.

He wanted to check on Grace but couldn't as he rounded the corner to find Logan facing off with two more males. Ren had to have Logan's back and be the wall of protection between the females and the threat that was coming.

He tried to aim for one of the males that Logan was fighting but it was too close. He swiveled as the four males from before rounded the corner and saw what was happening.

As one they all shifted into furry beasts resembling wolves—but nothing like Griff or any number of wolf shifters he knew.

These things were snarling, rabid beasts.

As two raced at him, and one at Logan—who'd just decapitated one of the males with his giant clawed paw—one disappeared from sight, likely thinking to circle around and attack.

Ren shot at the closest male, hit him in the arm, but the male kept coming.

He fired at the one behind him, but the male dodged, his reflexes fast.

So Ren fired again as they gained speed and slammed it directly into the thigh of the first one intentionally, then shot his other thigh. He needed these beasts incapacitated if he couldn't kill them immediately.

The beast screamed as the effects of the magical arrows took root. It fell on its back, its scream tearing through the air as Ren called on his jaguar, let the shift overcome him immediately.

He could hear the other male, saw him on the roof out of the corner of his eye. He let out a warning growl, hoped Logan understood as the male raced toward the edge of the roof in Logan's direction. In between the buildings was a perfect spot for an ambush.

Ren kept his focus on the beast lumbering at him, raced to the left, trying to lead it away from the females who were starting to stir.

Damn it, no. Don't move, don't draw attention to yourselves, he silently screamed.

Ren snarled, snapping his jaws at the male who started toward him, but then turned as Grace let out a groan of pain and sat up.

The rabid wolf creature headed in her direction, its snarls terrifying and deadly.

Grace let out a startled scream. Ren moved silently and jumped on the beast's back, opening his jaws wide and clamping down on its neck.

He tore through bone and cartilage, severing the head from its body even as Grace screamed again.

"Behind you!"

He reacted quickly, jumping off the body and swiveling around at the male he'd shot trying to attack.

The male was unsteady on his feet as he tried to fight the effects of the arrows.

Ren moved in low, clamped down hard on the male's ankle, earning a howl of pain while he quickly moved off him.

Then he darted around the male with the quickness of his jaguar nature and jumped on the beast's back, just as he had the other one.

The male tried to swat at him from the front, catching Ren's face with its claws as Ren clamped down on his neck and killed him exactly the same way he'd killed the other beast.

By the time he was done and turned back for another attack, Logan was limping toward him, now naked in human form, blood dripping from his hands.

Ren shifted quickly, breathing hard. "You good?"

"Yeah. This isn't my blood," Logan said and that was all Ren heard before he hurried to Grace's side, crouched in front of her. As he did, Koa started stirring.

"Are you injured?" He went to cup her face, realized he was covered in—blood and other things. He started wiping his hands on the grass.

"No...I don't think so." She blinked as if coming out of a daze. "Oh God, Ren, are you okay?" Not caring that he was covered in death, she threw herself at him, held him close.

He stood, bringing her with him even as Logan helped Koa to her feet. Ren's heart was damn near close to cracking. He could have lost her, but she was okay. Alive. His sweet, kind Grace was in his arms, her heart beating. He was going to be having nightmares for a while over this. "I'm fine. Oh goddess, Grace, I thought we'd lost you."

Impatient little chirps sounded and they all froze, saw that the dragonling had woken up too and was pissed to be tied up.

Logan let his claws extend, sliced right through what looked like magical netting, and they all worked to untangle the dragonling.

As soon as he was free, he raced away from them.

"Shit," Logan muttered, hurrying after him.

"You guys—" Ren was cut off.

"We're coming too," Grace said, both she and Koa hurrying forward, avoiding the dead bodies.

Ren cursed under his breath, yanked out a couple of his arrows as he ran after them and vowed to grab the rest later.

They all followed the dragonling to what turned out to be caged dragonlings even smaller than him and definitely undernourished. They cowered by the backs of their cages, their eyes wide as they made little chirping sounds.

"Oh, you poor babies." Grace stepped forward as Logan ripped the doors off the cages.

But Ren placed a hand in front of her. "They're scared and hungry. I'm not sure how they'll react."

"I hate that you're right," she murmured, leaning into him, still not caring that he was covered in blood. She wrapped her arms around him as Logan started cooing at the babies, trying to convince them to come out on their own. "They snuck up on us so fast and shoved something over our faces to knock us out."

"I've never been so scared in my life." Koa wrapped her arms around herself, the fear rolling off her equal to Grace's.

And Ren wished he could kill those males all over again.

"So what do we do now?" Grace murmured, looking up at him, shadows in her gaze.

"Get a crew in here, destroy the bodies completely and…" He looked over at Logan. "We'll probably have to do recon missions farther north now, make sure there aren't more of these things anywhere else."

"And we'll have to find safe homes for these babies," Grace added, looking over as Logan gently eased the first dragonling out of a cage.

Yeah, they would. But at least Grace was safe. That was the only thing he could fully process at the moment.

His female was alive, safe, and he was going to claim her. As soon as she would let him, he wanted to claim her forever.

CHAPTER SIXTEEN

When Grace opened her eyes in the apartment, she knew Ren was gone. He'd likely gone to get them breakfast—and the note on the bedside table confirmed it.

After the insanity of yesterday they'd cleaned up, then helped get the dragonlings settled into temporary situations. Then Ren had gone back to where they'd killed whatever those wolflike creatures had been and cleaned up everything—and they'd sent out scouts and trackers to do a thorough search of the surrounding area beyond to look for signs of life and more dragonlings.

She had no idea if they'd found anything because when Ren had finally gotten back they'd crashed hard. Still feeling sluggish, she made herself get up and shower, then brush her teeth, and basically just felt human again. Since it was Saturday, it was one of her days off and she planned to take advantage.

Hopefully with Ren, in bed. All day. Or most of it anyway.

After what had happened yesterday, she wasn't waiting another moment to have sex. She'd had this obsessive urge for everything to be perfect, but the reality was life wasn't perfect. And she knew that whatever happened with Ren, it would be perfect because it was him. He wouldn't be disappointed with her—also one of her fears. He might be older and more experienced, but when he looked at her…she knew he loved what he saw. He didn't want anyone but her.

As she emerged from the bathroom, a robe loosely tied around her waist, Ren stepped into their apartment, two coffee mugs and a big brown bag in hand.

"I brought breakfast and coffee."

"My hero," she said, laughing before taking that first sip of heaven.

His dark eyes sparked with lust. "It's ridiculous that I'm jealous of your coffee."

Which just made her snort-laugh. "It kind of is, but I still love you."

He froze, watching her with wide, dark eyes, the hints of amber sparking bright. "What?"

"I love you, Ren." She wondered if she should have held back, waited longer, but he'd saved her life—more than once, now that she thought about it—and he'd been showing up for her ever since he'd saved her from that vampire. Her family too. He was, simply put, perfect for her.

He set everything down and moved forward with that supernatural speed she still wasn't quite used to. After she set her own coffee down, he cupped her cheek gently, his eyes bright with hunger. "I've loved you for longer than I should admit. I will always love you and I know it's too soon to mate now, but I want you for my mate. Whenever you're ready for that next step, I'm all in. You and me, forever."

His words slammed into her, smoothed all the serrated edges of her fear that he might not feel the same. "Why is it too soon?" she whispered, leaning into his hold, wrapping her arms around him tight.

He blinked once. Twice. "You wish to mate. *Now?*"

She loved him and he loved her. Sometimes life was as simple as that. "I can't think of a better time. Life is too short, Ren. I don't want to have any 'what if' moments later. We love each other. I don't want to wait for something I know will be amazing. You're my home, Ren." And she couldn't imagine a world, her life, without him in it.

He swallowed hard, leaned his forehead against hers. "You own me, Grace. Completely."

They stood there for a long moment and she simply inhaled his dark, delicious scent, reveling in the fact that this was her male, her forever. The man smelled like rich coffee, her one weakness. Which made sense.

"Are we gonna get this show on the road or what?" she finally murmured into the quiet. Because being wrapped around him, feeling his hard, powerful body at her fingertips—she wanted all of this man. Now. Impatience was riding her hard, a tension coiled inside her that needed release.

He let out a startled laugh. He brushed his mouth over hers, his tongue exploring as he tugged on her robe's tie. "I love that I never know what's going to come out of your mouth. And I love..." He pushed the robe off her shoulders and let it pool to the floor. "The way you taste. So get on the bed, sweetheart."

A shiver rolled through her at his demanding tone. She'd quickly realized that her laid-back jaguar could be demanding and dominating in the bedroom. Which was insanely hot.

She crawled onto the bed, taking her time and enjoying the hiss of breath behind her as she slowly turned over, lay on her back, spread her legs.

She should feel vulnerable, but in that moment she felt powerful as his gaze swept over her. Heat curled through her, her nipples tightening in anticipation, her inner walls tightening around nothing, desperate to be filled by him.

The curtains were still drawn but there was enough daylight coming through them that he could easily see every inch of her. When she reached between her legs, touched her clit, he sucked in another breath before he moved into action.

"Nope," he murmured as he knelt between her spread thighs. "That's my job." He dipped his head even as she lifted her hips up to him. He licked once, slow and teasing. "And I take the job of making you come very seriously."

She slid her fingers through his dark hair, gripped his skull because she was about to combust from his stroking.

He eased a finger inside her, then two as he teased her clit in a steady rhythm, which reinforced just how quickly he'd learned her body.

And she understood him better now too. He was going to make sure she came at least once before he slid inside her. That was just the way he was wired. Her sweet, giving, deadly male. He was everything she never even imagined was possible.

She rolled her hips against his face as heat started to build inside her, that familiar sensation curling tight as he stroked his fingers inside her. Teased her clit.

When he sucked on the sensitive bundle of nerves, she suddenly surged into orgasm, her release punching through her in little waves of pleasure.

"Ren!" She dug her fingers into his head, not worried she'd hurt him.

As he withdrew his fingers, he watched her while he sucked on them, heat wild in his gaze.

She shoved up, ready to slowly undress him, but her male moved fast, taking off everything before he crawled onto the bed, his erection thick and hard.

Ren thought he probably should have gone slower undressing, but he couldn't hide his desperation for Grace. Not now. Hell, not ever. He'd needed to make sure she came first before they fully mated, before they crossed that line.

He still couldn't believe she was ready to mate, had thought he'd need to be patient—had been prepared for it.

But then she'd blurted out that she loved him.

His sweet, giving human wanted to mate him and he wasn't waiting another day. Another moment. She was right, life was far too short. Even with his longer life span he understood that.

Things happened so quickly, the whole direction of your life could change—or end—in a split second. Hell, his had the moment he'd met Grace.

As she wrapped her fingers around his cock he froze, forced himself to breathe as she stroked him hard.

Goddess, she understood what he needed already. But her hand wasn't what he was interested in right now.

He grasped her wrist, then took her other one and held them above her head as he lowered his mouth to hers, claimed her.

She teased her tongue against his, arching her back into him so that her breasts brushed against his chest.

The feel of her hard nipples against him had his balls pulling up tight. The mere fact that Grace was naked and underneath him was enough to get him rock hard.

"You're sure you want this?" he growled against her mouth, even as his jaguar swiped at him, told him to shut the fuck up.

She bit his bottom lip. "I'm going to pretend you didn't ask me that. You're mine, Ren."

His chest expanded at her words, at the way she was claiming him. He'd been so hurt in the past, had thought his heart had been broken forever. But it hadn't been. Not truly. Now Grace was the only one with the power to hurt him and he knew in his soul she never would.

"I'll have to bite you," he murmured, nipping her back.

"I know."

He'd figured she understood some of the mating stuff since her sister was mated to a shifter, but he hadn't wanted to shock her as he bit her— while she was coming.

Releasing her wrists, he cupped her breasts, teased her hard nipples slowly, sensually as he took his time kissing her.

She'd wrapped her legs around his waist and he could feel how wet she was against his cock. But he was forcing himself to show some control before he thrust into her. Because once that happened—

She lifted up slightly, angled her body so that her opening was right at his cock, and rolled her hips down on him.

He sucked in a breath as he sank deep inside her. "So. Tight." The only two words he managed to get out before she clutched onto his ass, silently demanding he move.

He lost all sense of time as he thrust inside her, explored her mouth, touched every exposed inch he could because he wanted all of her. And after this he planned to kiss every inch of her, to learn all of her body. Luckily they had forever in front of them.

As her inner walls started tightening, he knew she was close—and he'd barely been hanging on from the moment he'd pushed inside her.

He kissed a path down her jaw and neck, lightly nipped at the sensitive point between her neck and shoulder. When he did, her inner walls tightened again.

Oh, she liked that.

So he did it again even as he reached between their bodies and gently rubbed her clit. That opened the floodgates.

She jerked against him, her inner walls convulsing around him now as she began that free fall into pleasure.

He released his canines, the instinct taking over like a tempest as he sank them into the curve of her shoulder.

She cried out, her fingernails digging into his back, and he let go, coming hard inside her as she kept climaxing, her heat surrounding him as he found the sweetest release.

He quickly sealed up the tiny wounds he'd made, licking where he'd bit before he gently kissed the spot.

"That was amazing," she said through rasping breaths. "It's like... something clicked into place." She cupped his face, her expression one of pure joy.

A sense of awe slid through him. He felt it, but she was human; he hadn't been sure she'd experience the same thing. "It's the mating bond." He rolled over slightly but held her close, needing that skin to skin. Would be needing it from now until...always. "And we're just getting started, sweetheart."

EPILOGUE

One month later

"I t feels a little weird to be home," Grace murmured as Ren pulled into the driveway of her family's home.

"Good weird?" He shot her a sideways glance.

"Definitely. But...still weird. And I realized that we haven't even talked about where, ah..." She cleared her throat and glanced in the back seat where Griff was dozing. It still amazed her that he could just drop off at any moment and sleep like the dead.

"What?" Ren turned off the engine and took her hand, brushed his mouth over her knuckles.

"Are you going to move in here or will I move in with you?" Because she had no doubt that they'd be living together. She wouldn't be letting him sleep any nights away from her and knew he felt the same. But of all the things they'd discussed over the last month—and the tons of sex they'd been having—they'd never talked about what happened after their assignment.

"He's moving in here," Griff answered from the back, his eyes snapping open as he unstrapped and slid from the vehicle to stretch his legs.

"Why, thank you for answering for me," Ren grumbled to a retreating Griff, who'd already shut the door behind him.

These two really were like brothers. She bit back a laugh. "Is he right?"

He shrugged. "I kind of just assumed I'd unpack here and then grab the rest of my stuff later and bring it over. Unless you want to move in with Griff and Hyacinth? They keep later hours than you're used to and...I didn't think you'd want to be separated from your sisters."

God, she loved this male. "I'll be happy wherever you want to live. Maybe later we could even get our own place?" Things were different since The Fall. Multiple generations of families lived together in many cases because it was simply easier. There had been a housing shortage for a while and sometimes they still felt the crunch of that.

"I'm happy if you're happy. And if I'm being honest, I love your nana's cooking—so spending all our time in bed with you and eating like a king? Living here will not be a hardship."

She laughed at his blunt honesty. "Okay, good. I hate the thought of leaving my family right now." In the future she wanted a place that was just theirs—and hopefully some kids. Or maybe cubs. She wasn't sure exactly how all that would work. The only thing she knew for certain was now that she was mated to a supernatural and he'd claimed her, her own life expectancy would match his. "And, oh my God, we didn't even tell them about the dragonling." Her eyes widened as she stared at Ren.

He simply snickered. "What the hell have we been doing the past month?" he murmured before he opened his door. And moving quickly, he rounded the SUV and opened hers.

His question was definitely rhetorical. Because apart from work, all they'd done was have sex. Constant sex. In the morning, during their lunch breaks, at night. Apparently the mating instinct was no joke. Not that she had any complaints, but she couldn't believe she hadn't even thought to tell her family about the rescued dragonling she'd offered to keep for a while. Hopefully forever.

"I don't actually think they'll mind, but..." Grace trailed off as the front door flew open and her Nana Josephine, Jo and Luna and Cas all ran out to greet them.

Tears of joy stung her eyes as she found herself enveloped in hug after hug.

Even Cas hugged her tight—then clapped Ren ridiculously hard on the back as he said, "Congratulations on mating!"

Now *that* she hadn't forgotten to tell her family about. She'd pretty much told anyone who would listen how ridiculously happy and mated she was.

"We've planned a big celebration for you two," her nana said. "And we've already prepared your room. That sweet Hyacinth helped bring over your things already, Ren."

Okay, well, her family was far more prepared than them, which was amazing. "We also have some news—"

"Oh my God, you're pregnant!" Luna squealed.

"Wait, what? No!" Or she didn't think she was. They'd talked about it and…they weren't trying to wait or anything. She guessed she could be… Oh God, she wouldn't go there now. "We might have offered to house a dragonling for a while. She was part of a group of injured, captured dragonlings, and since you're a vet," she said to Jo, cursing herself for being such a sex-crazed scatterbrain, "and since Cas is a dragon…"

"A dragonling!" Jo's eyes went all mushy, and when Grace looked at the rest of them she knew it wasn't going to be a problem at all.

"We're not temporarily housing her. We're keeping her," Luna decided. "Where is she?"

Grace looked past them at the SUV and Griff, who'd shifted to his wolf form and was actually snoozing on the lawn in a patch of sunlight. *Freaking wolves.* "On her way. She can't fly for long periods of time or very far, but she'll be transported along with her siblings, later this afternoon. We're keeping them all relatively close to each other."

"Siblings?" Jo's eyes lit up.

"We're not keeping more than one dragonling," Nana said, laughing. "Now come inside, you two. It's been too long and I need time with my girl and her new mate." She gave Ren another squeeze before patting his cheek gently, tears glistening in her eyes. "I'm so happy to have you officially in the family."

"I'll grab your stuff," Cas said, literally shooing them inside. "And Griff will help with the bags too," he called out loudly to the wolf, who simply swished his tail in acknowledgement.

"I had so much fun, but it's good to be home," Grace said to Ren as they headed inside, their arms wrapped around each other.

"It really is," he murmured, leaning down to kiss her. "And for the record, my home is wherever you are."

She had to fight more tears of joy because she felt his words bone-deep. He was her forever, her home, her mate.

—THE END—

Dear Readers,

Thank you for reading Ancient Sentinel! If you'd like to stay in touch and be the first to learn about new releases you can:

- Check out my website for book news: https://www.katiereus.com
- Follow me on Bookbub: https://www.bookbub.com/profile/katie-reus
- Follow me on TikTok: https://www.tiktok.com/@katiereusauthor

Also, please consider leaving a review at one of your favorite online retailers. It's a great way to help other readers discover new books and I appreciate all reviews.

Happy reading,
Katie

ACKNOWLEDGMENTS

Thank you to Kaylea Cross for being the best critique partner! Sarah, thank you for all your behind-the-scenes work; Julia, thank you again for thorough edits and being flexible with your schedule. I'm also grateful to Jaycee for all her fabulous design work. For my readers, you guys are the best and I'm so thankful you still want to read my stories.

ABOUT THE AUTHOR

Katie Reus is the *New York Times* and *USA Today* bestselling author of the Red Stone Security series, the Ancients Rising series and the MacArthur Family series. She fell in love with romance at a young age thanks to books she pilfered from her mom's stash. Years later she loves reading romance almost as much as she loves writing it.

However, she didn't always know she wanted to be a writer. After changing majors many times, she finally graduated summa cum laude with a degree in psychology. Not long after that she discovered a new love. Writing. She now spends her days writing paranormal romance and sexy romantic suspense. If you would like to be notified of future releases, please visit her website: https://katiereus.com and join her newsletter.

COMPLETE BOOKLIST

Ancients Rising

Ancient Protector

Ancient Enemy

Ancient Enforcer

Ancient Vendetta

Ancient Retribution

Ancient Vengeance

Ancient Sentinel

Ancient Warrior

Ancient Guardian

Darkness Series

Darkness Awakened

Taste of Darkness

Beyond the Darkness

Hunted by Darkness

Into the Darkness

Saved by Darkness

Guardian of Darkness

Sentinel of Darkness

A Very Dragon Christmas

Darkness Rising

Redemption Harbor Series®

Resurrection

Savage Rising

Dangerous Witness

Innocent Target

Hunting Danger

Covert Games

Chasing Vengeance

Sin City Series (the Serafina)

First Surrender

Sensual Surrender

Sweetest Surrender

Dangerous Surrender

Deadly Surrender

Verona Bay Series

Dark Memento

Deadly Past

Silent Protector

Linked books

Retribution

Tempting Danger

Non-series Romantic Suspense

Running From the Past

Dangerous Secrets

Killer Secrets

Deadly Obsession

Danger in Paradise

His Secret Past

Paranormal Romance

Destined Mate

Protector's Mate

A Jaguar's Kiss

Tempting the Jaguar

Enemy Mine

Heart of the Jaguar